DON'T
TELL A SOUL

Rafael Shamay

Dedicated to my family and to all the good people who accompanied me on this journey.

Chapter 1

The night was dark and ominous. The sky seemed blacker and more forbidding than ever. Flashing lights cut through the gloom. Sirens wailed, echoing through the streets, drawing the attention of curious passersby.

The ambulance's sirens urged cars to clear the way on the congested, traffic-clogged roads.

Keren sat in the back, next to the paramedic, her eyes fixed on her friend Hezi, who lay unconscious on the stretcher. A bandage wrapped his head, darkened by a growing bloodstain.

Keren was shattered, shocked, and in pain.

Anxiety, terror, and fear gripped her.

She stayed mostly silent during the ride, tears streaming down her cheeks.

Her world had crumbled in an instant. Just yesterday, her life had been full of hope for a shared future, and now everything had shattered into pieces.

Had she lost the most precious thing in her life? She had to cling to hope, no matter what.

The ambulance screeched to a halt at the entrance of Ichilov Hospital in Tel Aviv. The doors swung open as a team of nurses and a doctor rushed a gurney toward the vehicle.

Dr. Snir shouted, "On three, we lift together! Understood?"

The team nodded, each gripping a side of the critically injured patient. They carefully lifted him and placed him on the gurney.

"Take him to the operating room," Dr. Snir ordered.

The team hurriedly wheeled the gurney inside, with Dr. Snir close behind.

Keren hurried out of the vehicle, doing her best to keep up with the team pushing the gurney before they disappeared down the hospital corridors.

"Move aside!" Dr. Snir shouted at curious onlookers who lingered at the sight of the team escorting the injured man.

Suddenly, Dr. Snir noticed Keren, whom he hadn't seen until that moment.

"Who are you?" he asked impatiently.

"I'm his girlfriend," she replied.

"Wait in the visitor's room, and we'll update you on his condition later."

The gurney passed by the reception desk, where clerks and nurses sat watching them with curiosity.

"Locate his family and call for an anesthesiologist immediately," Dr. Snir shouted at them, continuing on his way without waiting for an answer.

The operating room doors burst open, and the gurney, along with the entire team, disappeared inside.

Keren sat alone in the lobby, waiting anxiously for news about the surgery. She looked exhausted, scared, helpless, somewhat detached, but mostly worried about her boyfriend's well-being. She wiped away the tears streaming down her cheeks.

The receptionist noticed her and walked over, offering a glass of water.

"Here," she said kindly. "The social worker will come soon to check on you."

"When will I know how he's doing?" Keren asked.

"Only when the surgery is over. It might take many hours. We're all praying for his recovery and for the surgery to be successful."

Keren lowered her gaze, silent.

"I believe he'll be okay," the receptionist added, before returning to her desk.

People passed by, some casting curious glances, while others ignored her completely.

A short while later, the social worker arrived.

"Hello, my name is Mira. I'll keep you company. You can share whatever's on your mind or anything that's troubling you."

Keren chose to remain silent; she had been through too much in one day and didn't feel like talking.

Mira understood, pulled out a business card, and handed it to Keren.

"This is the phone number for the Victims of Hostilities Association. They provide psychological and legal advice and will explain the rights you're entitled to. Everything is free of charge."

Keren took the card and said, "Thank you."

Mira left, and Keren was alone again.

The hours dragged on, each one feeling like a year.

It was late. The hospital was emptied of visitors and now resembled an abandoned, desolate building. Patients' groans echoed through the halls, some calling out for a nurse's help, praying she would arrive quickly.

Keren approached the receptionist, hoping for an update, but there was no new information.

"We'll let you know as soon as we hear anything," she promised.

Hope turned to despair, then back to hope, over and over again.

Fatigue overcame her, and Keren fell into a deep sleep, her head resting against the wall.

After what felt like an eternity, Dr. Snir finished the complex surgery.

"Transfer him to the intensive care unit," he said as he stepped out of the operating room.

Dr. Snir looked drained and weary. It had been one of the most challenging surgeries of his career. He changed his clothes and went to the reception desk for more information.

"Did you manage to find his parents?" he asked curiously.

"He doesn't have parents; he's an orphan," the receptionist replied.

"No other family?"

"No. His girlfriend is here," she said, pointing to the girl asleep in the waiting room.

Dr. Snir approached Keren and gently touched her shoulder.

Keren woke with a start from a dream she couldn't remember.

"I'm the doctor who operated on Hezi."

"How is he, Doctor?" she asked, trying to focus.

"It's hard to say. Right now, we're trying to stabilize him. We removed two bullets from the back of his skull and managed to stop the bleeding in his brain. I can't promise you he'll make it. He may not wake up at all, or he could fall into a coma. If he does wake up, he could be paralyzed for the rest of his life—or worse, he may not survive. It's too early to tell. I'd advise you not to get your hopes up, though it's not really my place to say."

"Doctor, can I see him?"

"Not right now. It's better if you go home and rest. We'll update you on any changes, for better or worse."

"I'm done with my shift. I can give you a ride home or call you a taxi, whichever you prefer."

"I'd rather you take me home," she said, lowering her gaze to the ground in despair.

"Alright, let's go. My car is parked around the back of the building."

Keren got up from her seat and followed him. When they reached his car, she was surprised to see that it was simple, old, and not as luxurious as she had imagined.

Dr. Snir pressed the remote, unlocked the door, got in, and sat in the driver's seat. Keren followed and sat beside him.

He started the car, turned on the radio, tuned it to soft music, and began to drive.

"Where to?" he asked, opening an app on his phone.

"12 Arlozorov Street," she replied.

Dr. Snir entered the address and continued driving.

She stayed silent the entire way, her mind racing with thoughts.

Would Hezi make it? Would she have to visit him in the hospital every day for a long time? Would he be paralyzed for life?

Dr. Snir didn't want to add to her burden. She'd been through a traumatic day, so he remained silent as well. The heavy quiet filled the car until they reached her home.

"Thank you, Doctor," she said, hurriedly exiting the car and quickly making her way inside.

She entered her house quietly, without turning on the light, to avoid waking anyone. Her mother, who had been worried, sat on the couch in the living room, anxiously awaiting her return.

It was three in the morning. In a few short hours, daylight would break, erasing the horrors of the previous night and leaving some with painful scars and lingering fears.

"Where were you? I was worried about you," her mother asked, suddenly approaching as Keren closed the door behind her.

"I was with Hezi," she replied, without elaborating.

"Is everything okay? You came home late," her mother asked, still concerned.

"Yes. No. I don't want to talk about it," Keren answered, heading to her room, leaving her mother watching as she walked away.

Keren closed her door, lay down on her bed still in her clothes, and struggled to fall asleep.

The horrors of the night replayed in her mind, relentless and more intense than ever.

Dawn broke, and the street outside came to life. Her parents left for work, leaving her alone. Loneliness and anguish consumed her, dragging her into the abyss, into the threatening darkness.

Keren felt paralyzed; she could barely get out of bed and drag herself to the bathroom. Every little noise startled her, every sound beyond the door from the bustling street seemed to threaten to awaken the dormant demons inside her soul.

She returned to her room, shut the door, and crawled back into bed, trying to escape the terror of life.

For most of the day, Keren stayed in her room, lying in bed, frozen with fear. Her heart raced, and beads of sweat formed on her forehead.

Memories of the previous night's horrors surfaced again and again, giving her no peace, battering her like relentless waves.

Sarit's mother—Keren's mother—returned from work in the early afternoon and found Keren still locked in her room.

"Keren, are you okay?" she asked from behind the door.

"Everything's fine," Keren lied. But when Sarit invited her to eat, she refused to come out. Only in the early evening did she gather the strength to get up, drink some water, and eat a little. When Sarit tried to get her to talk and open up, Keren shut herself off and quickly returned to her room, locking the door behind her.

The nights were unforgiving. Keren would dream and wake up in a panic, sitting upright in bed, staring into the darkness of the room, sweating and frightened. For a long time, she tried to stay awake, afraid that if she closed her eyes, the nightmares would torment her again. The moonlight streaming through the windowpanes cast threatening shadows of the objects scattered around the room. Keren ignored them, and finally, sheer exhaustion would take over, and she'd fall asleep for the rest of the night.

Whenever her parents tried to get her to open up, she pushed them away and escaped to her room.

Sarit, however, didn't give up. She knew that if she turned a blind eye or, heaven forbid, ignored the situation, Keren's distress would worsen, leading to a serious decline in her mental state. A few days passed, and Keren's mental health did deteriorate, just as her mother had feared.

One morning, when Keren came out of her room to use the bathroom, Sarit seized the opportunity, slipping into her room and quietly waiting on her bed. When Keren returned, she was startled to find her mother there, looking alarmed.

"Come, sit next to me. I don't bite," Sarit said with a smile. Keren reluctantly sat beside her.

"I'm your mother; you can tell me anything." At that, Keren broke down, tears pouring from her eyes. Sarit pulled her into a tight embrace.

"It's okay. Let it all out; you'll feel better afterward."

Keren sobbed, and when she finally calmed down, she started telling her mother about the events of that dark Saturday night. When she finished, Sarit looked horrified.

"That's awful. I had no idea you were there," she said, then asked, "How is he?"

"I don't know. He's in intensive care, and they wouldn't let me in."

"Let's hope he pulls through," Sarit replied, then added gravely, "The important thing is that you're safe and healthy, but you really need to see a professional, a psychologist. This is a serious trauma. You can't ignore it."

"The social worker at the hospital gave me this." Keren took out a business card from her pocket and showed it to her mother.

"Do you want me to call her?" Sarit asked, her concern deepening.

"No, I'll call."

"Alright. Call her today—don't put it off."

"Okay," Keren replied.

Sarit left the room, deeply worried about her daughter's health, and hurried to update her husband, Yotam. He seemed surprised, trying to gather as many details as possible from his wife.

"I saw it on the news; it was a terrible incident. I never imagined she was there," he responded anxiously. "What are we going to do?"

"She'll meet with a psychologist, and we'll see how things progress."

Chapter 2

Keren called the "Returning to Life" organization with great trepidation. A woman answered on the other end, took her details, and scheduled an appointment with Yoni, a psychologist.

> "We at the organization will support you and advise you as much as needed. You're in good hands; there's no need to worry," the woman reassured her.

When Tuesday arrived, Keren left the house accompanied by her mother. It was cold and raining—weather she didn't like. Winter always made her sad; she much preferred sunny days. Sarit opened the umbrella to shield them as they walked toward the nearby parked car.

Sarit opened the door, letting Keren get in first while holding the umbrella over her. She closed the door and quickly made her way to the driver's seat, folding the umbrella before starting the car and driving toward the city center.

Keren remained silent and withdrawn the entire ride. Even the voice of the radio announcer didn't register in her mind. Sarit occasionally glanced at her with worried eyes but chose not to break the silence.

The rain had stopped, but dark clouds still hung overhead, threatening to release another downpour at any moment. When they arrived at a tall, gray building with dark windows, Sarit said, "We're here. Call me when you're done, and I'll come pick you up."

"Okay, Mom," Keren replied, hesitantly stepping out of the car and walking toward the building's entrance.

On the seventh floor, Keren saw a glass door with the organization's name, "Returning to Life." She opened it slowly.

"Are you Keren?" the receptionist asked, noticing her as she looked around the reception hall.

"Yes," Keren answered, walking over to her.

"Dr. Gordon is waiting for you in his office," the receptionist said, pointing to a nearby door.

With great apprehension, Keren opened the office door and peeked inside.

"Come in," Dr. Gordon smiled, inviting her in.

The office had an old-fashioned look. It wasn't the kind of room she had imagined—there was no couch. A gloomy landscape painting hung on the white wall, and a wooden desk stood in front of an older man with gray hair. The blinds on the window overlooking the busy street were closed, and the room was dimly lit.

Keren sat down in the chair opposite him and lowered her gaze.

"How are you?" he asked gently.

"I'm okay," she replied, looking up to meet his eyes.

"I want you to know that we're here to help, and everything you say will stay between us," he assured her.

Keren nodded but said nothing.

"There's a coffee corner if you'd like something to drink," Dr. Gordon said, pointing to a small table in the corner of the office with boxes of sugar, tea, coffee, and a hot water kettle.

"No, thank you," she replied politely.

"Let's start from the beginning," he said, his face growing serious. "Tell me a little about yourself."

"There's not much to tell. My name is Keren. I finished studying architecture and interior design. Right now, I'm working a temporary job at a clothing store."

"Do you have any hobbies?"

"I mostly listen to music, read books, and watch movies. Not much else."

"Do you have a partner?" he asked.

"Yes," she replied, lowering her gaze again.

"Tell me a little about your partner. What's his name?"

"His name is Hezi," she said, hesitating before continuing. "Hezi is full of life and funny. He mainly loves working with computers."

"How did you meet him?"

Keren smiled. "It happened a few months ago. Hezi was going through a tough time. His mother was terminally ill, and he had to leave his job to take care of her. Before we started dating, he had been seeing other women, but he couldn't form serious relationships, and his mother's illness put an end to his attempts.

After a long struggle, his mother passed away. Hezi was devastated. He was left alone in the world..."

"Where's his father?" Dr. Gordon interrupted.

"His father was killed in the war when Hezi was about a year old. He doesn't remember him, just has a few family photos from happier times."

"That must have been hard for him," Gordon remarked.

"Yes. His mother's death left a huge void, and there were also debts—mainly water and electricity bills."

"He must have inherited something," Gordon noted.

"Just the old apartment. His mother was a pensioner living on a stipend, and she didn't have any savings."

Gordon looked at her deeply, pondering how to continue. "So, Hezi was left alone," he finally said.

"Yes. Of course, he mourned her, and for a month, he couldn't do anything. It took him a while to pick up the pieces and move on. He needed to find a new job to start supporting himself and pay off the debts."

Gordon glanced at the clock on the wall. An hour had passed in the blink of an eye. He smiled at her and said, "Time... time flies too fast. Time is a precious commodity. If I could buy more time, I'd get so much more done. But unfortunately, that's not possible. Shall we meet on Thursday?"

"Yes," she replied.

"Thursday at five, then," he confirmed.

Keren stood up, said goodbye to Gordon, and left his office. She called her mother, asking her to come pick her up. Keren waited on the street for about twenty minutes until Sarit arrived, navigating through the heavy traffic.

When she pulled up near the entrance, she rolled down the window. "Come on, get in."

Keren got in, closed the door, and settled into her seat.

"How was the meeting?" Sarit asked curiously.

"It was fine," Keren replied, not offering any further details.

"Would you like to go visit Hezi in the hospital?"

Keren was overwhelmed with emotions, and the thought of seeing Hezi again made her feel vulnerable. She wasn't sure she could handle it. But after a moment of reflection, she said, "Okay, let's go to the hospital."

When they arrived, they inquired at the reception desk about Hezi's room. The receptionist typed his name into the system and looked at the screen.

"He's in intensive care, on the 5th floor," she said.

They got into the elevator and reached the fifth floor. After asking for further directions, they continued down a narrow corridor, entered the department, and cautiously approached the room where Hezi was hospitalized.

Keren entered slowly, bracing herself for the worst. Hezi lay in bed, unconscious and connected to a ventilator. A large, blood-stained bandage covered his head. Sarit followed her, standing beside her daughter and looking at Hezi with compassion. She placed a comforting hand on Keren's shoulder and pulled her into a hug.

Keren sat down in the chair next to Hezi's bed and took his hand. Tears streamed down her face. She remained there for a long time, lost in the silence that filled the room—whether from shock or discomfort, she couldn't tell.

Sarit gently touched her shoulder again. "It's time to go," she whispered.

"Hezi, can you hear me?" Keren asked, hoping for a miracle, but there was no response.

Reluctantly, she stood up and left the room with her mother. Her heart was heavy with sadness, but deep down, she clung to the hope of better days ahead.

On the way home, Sarit said quietly, "I find it hard to believe he'll recover. And even if he does, he'll likely be disabled or paralyzed for the rest of his life."

"He will recover. I can feel it," Keren insisted.

"I think you should move on."

"I'm not going to leave Hezi alone. He needs me, and I love him," Keren said angrily.

"You two have only been together for barely three months," her mother pointed out.

"And they were the most beautiful moments of my life."

"I'm just saying..." Sarit began, but she fell silent when she saw Keren turn away and stare out the window, detached.

Sarit believed Keren was making a mistake with Hezi. There was no real future in this relationship. Even if he woke up, he would likely remain disabled and dependent for the rest of his life. Why should Keren have to endure that? She was still young, with her whole life ahead of her. She could meet someone else, fall in love again, and build a family.

As these thoughts raced through Sarit's mind while she drove, she chose to remain silent, for now.

Chapter 3

Keren still couldn't return to work, knowing it was only a matter of time before someone else took her place, and indeed, it happened. She told herself she would find another job in the future, something better, more rewarding, perhaps closer to home. But for now, Hezi was more important. He was hospitalized, helpless, in critical condition, and needed her—or so she thought.

Keren continued to isolate herself in her room; the world outside still seemed threatening and scary, full of dangers. All of Sarit's attempts to get her out for some fresh air or to go anywhere were in vain.

A week passed, and Hezi's condition remained unchanged, but Keren didn't lose hope and continued to visit him frequently, much to her mother's dismay.

On Monday, she scheduled another meeting with Dr. Gordon, the psychologist. She wasn't enthusiastic about these sessions, but they were necessary to relieve the burden, confront her fears, and speak with a professional who could help her process the weight of what she had experienced and its implications.

Once again, Sarit drove her to Gordon's office. And once again, Keren entered with a growing sense of apprehension, worried that perhaps this session might do more harm than good.

"Come in, have a seat," he said with a forced smile.

Keren sat down across from him and looked directly at him.

"How are you feeling?" he asked.

"Fine," she replied briefly.

"Would you like something to drink?"

"No."

"Let's continue. So, Hezi found a new job... what is it, by the way?"

"Programming at a high-tech company," she answered.

"They pay well in high-tech," he commented with a chuckle.

"He didn't complain and worked long hours."

"How did you two meet?"

"After Hezi found that job and was content, he decided it was time to start a new relationship. He joined social networks, saw my profile, and contacted me mainly through messages. After a month, we decided to meet at 'Georgie's' restaurant on the boardwalk, by the beach."

"How was the meeting?"

"I met a special person. Smart, sensitive, and considerate."

"Sounds perfect," he commented.

"He was a bit shy, introverted. But we quickly formed a special connection, a friendship."

"Let's move forward. So, you dated for a few months, and your relationship deepened. Tell me about the day before the traumatic event."

"That day, we planned to celebrate my birthday at 'Sitra,' a restaurant in the Sarona complex. It's a colorful place with restaurants and shops, always full of people. I bought new clothes especially for the occasion and even went to the hairdresser to get my hair done.

We planned to meet at seven in the evening. Hezi arrived on time to pick me up—he was always punctual. He opened the car door for me and smiled. I even remember the song that was playing on the radio as the car began to move.

All the way, we talked about what it feels like to be twenty-five and our plans for the future. I was happy.

We reached the complex after a short twenty-minute drive. Hezi parked in the nearby parking lot, and we walked into the complex. We arrived at the restaurant and saw a few couples waiting in line at the entrance. The hostess greeted us, checked her list to see if we had a reservation, and then let us in. A young waiter escorted us to our reserved table, seated us, and handed us the menu."

"Did you notice anything unusual? Something suspicious?" Gordon interrupted.

"No, not at that moment," she answered.

"Continue."

"The waiter returned with our order and placed it on the table."

Keren suddenly fell silent, as if frozen.

"We can continue another day if it's too difficult for you," he offered.

"No, it's okay."

"Shall I get you a glass of water?"

"Yes, thank you," she replied politely.

Keren drank thirstily from the glass, then continued speaking.

"As we were eating, two men entered, dressed in black suits and white shirts, wearing black ties, and holding black designer bags. They walked in and sat down to our right. They looked calm and composed..."

"Yet they caught your attention," he interrupted.

"Yes. Most of the people in the restaurant were couples who had come to enjoy themselves, but these men looked different, both in their attire and behavior."

"What do you mean?"

"While everyone else was talking, laughing, and absorbed in their own world, they sat silently, observing their surroundings."

"Go on."

"Hezi was telling me about his experiences at work and the activities he enjoyed. I smiled and listened, occasionally sneaking a glance at the two men in black suits.

We finished eating and had just started drinking the beverages we had ordered. The men then lifted their bags from the floor and placed them on the table. As we continued our conversation, they took out guns from the bags.

They shouted loudly, 'Allahu Akbar' (God is Great in Arabic), stood up from their chairs, and began shooting at the diners indiscriminately. It all happened so fast.

I watched the shooters approaching me and was momentarily paralyzed. I heard screams and horrifying cries all around. Those who could, got up from their chairs and began to flee in all directions, running for their lives.

Hezi turned his head to the side since he was facing away from the shooters. One of the gunmen fired two bullets into his head, and he collapsed, his head hitting the table, blood streaming.

I quickly got up and managed to escape in the nick of time. I ran as fast as I could toward the restroom while others ran outside, crying for help. Those who didn't manage to escape were shot dead.

I opened the restroom stall quickly, and soon two other women pushed in. We closed the door behind us, and the three of us sat on the floor, crouched, trembling with fear and horror. We continued to hear gunfire and screams from inside the restaurant. Then suddenly, there was silence. We heard voices speaking in Arabic that we didn't understand, followed by footsteps approaching us. Shortly after, we heard gunfire again, this time outside the restaurant, and then silence once more. We heard crying and screaming. Then we heard a few men speaking in Hebrew, trying to calm the wounded."

We heard them say, "It's over; you're safe now."

We came out of the restroom, terrified, and saw the counter-terrorism unit in the restaurant. Rescue forces were everywhere. Bodies lay on the floor, lifeless—a real massacre. A horrifying sight. The floor was covered in pools of blood.

I stood there, helpless.

Suddenly, I saw Hezi lying on a stretcher. I screamed and tried to run to him, but one of the paramedics blocked me. "He's alive," he said seriously and pushed the stretcher out

They began evacuating the wounded and the dead. I begged to join him in the ambulance, and they let me. That's how I got to the hospital.

"How is his condition?" Gordon asked.

"He's in very serious, possibly critical condition. He's on a ventilator and sedated. He's not responding to his surroundings."

Gordon sensed Keren's distress. He stood from his chair and handed her a glass of water.

She drank thirstily. When she finished, she said, "Later, I was told it was two terrorists from a village in Judea and Samaria who came to attack Israel."

"Yes. They showed them on TV during the news bulletin, just minutes before they entered the restaurant. They were captured on security cameras—cold-blooded and determined," Gordon confirmed.

Keren looked at Gordon with a helpless expression.

"Our time is up. We'll continue next week."

Keren nodded in agreement, stood up, and left the office.

Sarit was waiting at the building's entrance. Keren got into the car without a word.

"How was it?" Sarit asked

"Okay," Keren replied, turning her gaze to the window.

Sarit didn't press her further, leaving her alone with her thoughts.

The car began to move. Keren was lost in thoughts of Hezi, the traumatic event that haunted her, the bleakness of the future, and the effort it took to maintain a semblance of normal life.

She barely noticed the distance they had covered, only realizing they had arrived home when the car stopped.

The vegetable soup and noodle dish Sarit served her in the kitchen offered some comfort after the exhausting day. When she finished eating, she retreated to her room, locked the door, and tried to process everything she had been through.

Chapter 4

Two weeks had passed since the traumatic event, and Keren still rarely left the house, spending most of her time secluded in her room. If she did go out, it was always with her mother, during the day, and close to home—usually just a short walk to get some fresh air.

One day, after gathering the courage to eat out with her mother at a neighborhood restaurant, Sarit took the opportunity to talk to her about the future.

"It's time for you to look for a job in your field. You need to get out of the house, meet people, and change your environment," she urged.

"I don't know. It feels too soon. I still haven't recovered," Keren hesitated.

"I understand, but finding a job takes time. It's better to start now than wait too long—it's for your own good. A change of scenery will help."

Keren's thoughts drifted to Hezi. She loved him, and it pained her to see him lying in the hospital, unconscious, hovering between life and death. How could she focus on work when all she could think about was him? Eventually, she reconsidered and realized her mother was right.

"Okay, I'll start looking."

"Great, that's progress," Sarit said, satisfied.

The next day, Keren opened the laptop on her desk and began searching for job openings on employment websites. The search was exhausting; many positions required work experience that Keren didn't have. She spent three hours in front of the screen, feeling a mix of frustration, hope, and disappointment.

Suddenly, she came across an opening at an architecture firm on the other side of the city that didn't require prior experience. She immediately emailed her resume. Later, she concluded that to improve her chances, she should apply for positions requiring experience as well. It couldn't hurt.

Keren tried not to get her hopes up. She knew that each desirable job would attract thousands of applicants, many with far more experience, making the odds feel stacked against her.

Around midday, she called a taxi to take her to the hospital to visit Hezi.

When she entered his room, there was still no sign of recovery. His head remained bandaged, though the wrappings were no longer stained with blood. Keren sat beside him and held his hand. Tears welled in her eyes, streaming down her cheeks. Hezi was the love of her life—she had imagined a future with him. Now, everything felt abruptly cut short, with no hope in sight. She felt like a broken vessel, hollowed out by sadness, her throat tight with unshed tears.

Dr. Snir entered the room to check on Hezi's condition. Keren watched in silence as the doctor examined the monitor and reviewed the medical chart.

"What's his condition, Doctor?" she finally mustered the courage to ask.

"Critical but stable," he answered.

"What does that mean?"

"It means he's still not out of danger, but his pulse has stabilized, even though he can't yet breathe on his own."

Dr. Snir left the room, and Keren stayed for about an hour, gazing at Hezi with compassion. "I won't leave you. I'll make sure you get better," she whispered in his ear. But deep down, she knew there was little she could do beyond offering moral support.

A stern-looking nurse entered and announced that visiting hours were ending, then hurried off to the next room. Keren gave Hezi one last sorrowful look, kissed his cheek, and whispered, "I have to go, but I'll visit you again." He gave no response. Keren rose from her chair, left the room, took a taxi, and returned home.

After completing his daily rounds, Dr. Snir returned to Hezi's room with the accompanying nurse, Smadar. "It seems his condition has stabilized, and he can breathe on his own," he told her. "Tomorrow, we'll disconnect him from the ventilator and see how he responds." Smadar nodded in agreement.

The next day, Dr. Snir entered the room with slight apprehension and disconnected the ventilator. To his relief, Hezi was able to breathe on his own. Satisfied, Dr. Snir made a note in the chart.

Meanwhile, Keren had begun receiving job offers and scheduled her first interview. She knew it wouldn't be easy—competition was fierce, and her lack of experience made it even harder. Even if she landed a job, the starting salary would likely be below industry standards, but she understood this as part of the process.

Keren attended her first interview, though it didn't go well. She kept applying and went to additional interviews. Some interviewers asked relevant professional questions, while others posed bizarre, unrelated ones—about her hobbies, cleanliness habits, or personal weaknesses. She answered patiently and with composure, but deep down, she suspected most of them wouldn't call back, despite their polite assurances.

When she returned home, her parents would always ask, "How was the job interview?"

Her answers were often the same: "It was okay," or "Let's hope for the best." Time dragged on, and each passing day without a call chipped away at her hope, replacing it with quiet despair.

Then one day, her phone rang. Keren answered, her heart racing.

"Keren?" a woman's voice asked, confirming she had the right person.

"Yes," Keren replied, curiosity piqued.

"You've been accepted for a position at Horizons architecture firm. When can you start?"

"Tomorrow," Keren answered without hesitation.

"Perfect. Be there at nine in the morning. My name is Iris," the woman said before giving her the location details and ending the call.

A mix of joy and sadness washed over Keren—joy for the new beginning and sadness that Hezi wasn't part of it. He wouldn't be able to wish her success or wrap her in a reassuring hug, whispering that everything would be okay.

Despite her new job, Keren continued her weekly sessions with Gordon, her psychologist. It had been three weeks since the incident, but the memory still felt raw, as if it had happened only yesterday. She opened the door to Gordon's office, entered, and sat down.

"How are you feeling?" he asked with a warm smile.

"Okay," she answered briefly.

"And how was your week?"

"I found a new job and started working."

"That's great," he said encouragingly.

"But I'm still having bad dreams at night and struggling to fall asleep."

"Tell me about the dreams," he requested gently.

"Dreams about the dead and the wounded. About bad people."

"It will take time for those dreams to fade," Gordon reassured her. "The important thing is not to sink into despair. The fact that you've started working shows that you're moving forward."

Keren nodded in agreement.

"And what about Hezi?" Gordon asked.

"There's been no change," she replied, her voice heavy with despair.

Gordon fell silent, his concern for Hezi evident. He had hoped for a more hopeful update. "I hope he recovers soon," he said finally, though he didn't sound entirely convinced.

"I pray for him every day," Keren whispered.

"It's important not to lose hope," Gordon reminded her.

Keren nodded again, though doubt lingered in her heart.

Gordon sat quietly for a moment, contemplating Hezi's condition. He wondered whether waiting for him to recover would sustain Keren's hope or, in time, worsen her emotional state if hope eventually faded. Would holding on help her, or would it leave her shattered when she realized her waiting had been in vain?

He glanced at the clock on the wall to stay on schedule. "We have to finish," he said gently. "Same time next week?"

"Yes," Keren agreed. She rose from her chair, gave him a small nod, and left the office.

"Yes," she replied, rising from her chair, saying goodbye to Gordon before leaving his office.

Chapter 5

Dr. Snir arrived for his routine work shift. Nurse Yulia was waiting for him at the reception desk in the department.

"Good morning," she said with a smile.

"Good morning," he replied.

"Are you ready for the daily rounds?"

"Always."

The two of them went through the patient rooms in the department, reviewing their medical conditions. Yulia updated him on the treatments the patients had received during the previous shift. Dr. Snir listened, occasionally asking questions and adding his own comments.

When they reached the room where Hezi was, Yulia said, "There's no change in his condition. In my opinion, euthanasia would spare him from suffering."

Dr. Snir was taken aback by her response. "We're here to care for patients, not to kill them," he reprimanded her. "As long as there's even the slightest chance he might live, we will continue to treat him and hope for his recovery."

Yulia didn't want to argue and remained silent.

Professor Levin, the head of the department, seemed deep in thought. He glanced at the clock in annoyance; he didn't like it when people were late for the weekly Thursday meeting. Most of the doctors had already taken their seats around the table, waiting intently for his words.

As the last doctor entered, the meeting began. The doctors presented the issues they had encountered in the department: a shortage of equipment, lack of staff, long working hours at unusual times, and aggressive, irritable family members of patients

Suddenly, Levin turned to Dr. Snir. "You've been quiet until now. Is everything okay?"

"Yes. There's just one thing that's bothering me."

"Yes?"

"I have a patient in the department, his name is Hezi. He has been in a coma for several weeks. He was on a ventilator, but now he's breathing on his own. However, there's been no other change in his condition. He doesn't respond to his surroundings or react to stimuli. I'm worried that the damage he's suffered is irreversible."

"Did you send him for a brain scan?" Levin asked.

"No."

"So, what are you waiting for? Send him as soon as possible, and then we can assess his condition."

"Okay."

"Any other questions? Complaints? Requests?" Levin scanned the conference room with his authoritative gaze. There was a general silence.

"Alright. The meeting is adjourned," he said and left the room without another word.

Dr. Snir returned to the department, approached Yulia, and instructed, "Take Hezi for a brain scan. I want to see if there's any change from last time."

"Okay," she replied.

About two hours later, Yulia brought Hezi back to his room with a brown envelope. She left the room and began looking for Dr. Snir.

"Oh, there you are," she said when she spotted him in the corridor. "I brought you the scans," she added, handing him the envelope.

"Come with me to the office."

They entered his office, and Dr. Snir closed the door behind them. He sat at his desk, turned on the lamp, pulled the scans from the envelope, and examined them intently. Yulia sat across from him, waiting in silence.

"This is impossible," he muttered after a while.

"What?" she asked, curious.

"The area where the bullets penetrated is starting to heal."

Dr. Snir showed Yulia the scan, pointing to the injury site.

"Yes, it's healing," she replied cautiously. "But I'm not sure the damage hasn't already been done."

"The bullets hit at a certain angle. There's still a chance the damage is less severe than we feared," he said. "I need to show this to Professor Levin."

Yulia seemed less enthusiastic than Dr. Snir. From her experience, the chances of Hezi regaining normal function were slim, and she didn't see the point in getting her hopes up.

The shift ended. In the locker room, Dr. Snir changed out of his white uniform, preparing to head home. Yulia, also finished with her shift, approached him.

"Do you want to grab a drink?" she asked unexpectedly.

"After a grueling twenty-six-hour shift, I think I'll just sleep. Maybe another time."

Yulia looked a little disappointed, but she understood.

Meanwhile, Keren had started working at the architecture firm, and the job proved challenging. Despite the knowledge she had gained during her studies, she still had much to learn in practice: planning structures inside and out, situating them topographically, integrating them into the landscape, and solving technical issues according to legal requirements.

Keren immersed herself in exciting new projects and met interesting people. The job demanded her full involvement, sometimes requiring work at odd hours, but she managed to meet expectations and achieve her goals. Yet, most of the time, she remained withdrawn, often keeping to herself.

One persistent thought weighed on her mind—how happy and fulfilled she would feel if only she could share these new experiences and successes with Hezi.

But to her deep sorrow, Hezi showed no sign of awareness or response. He couldn't share in her joy or console her struggles. Tears welled up in her eyes. She looked around to ensure no one noticed, then quickly wiped them away.

Chapter 6

Keren arrived at the hospital in the afternoon to see if there had been any improvement in Hezi's condition. Her mother often tried to convince her to let go, insisting repeatedly that Hezi wouldn't survive his injuries, and that Keren needed to move on with her life.

But how could she move on? She loved him. Besides, the dreams, the horrific memories, the fears—they clung to her relentlessly, threatening to pull her into a dark abyss.

In the corridor, she ran into Dr. Snir, who was on his way to the ward.

"How is Hezi, Doctor?" she asked.

"I have good news. The head injury is healing remarkably well. But unfortunately, he still isn't responding to stimuli."

"In other words?"

"In other words, he's still unconscious, and we don't know if he'll ever wake up. But we need to hope for the best."

"Yes, definitely," she replied.

Keren said goodbye and walked into Hezi's room. He lay in bed just as she had seen him during her previous visits. This time, however, the bandage that had wrapped around his head was gone. She noticed the injured area—bare, with no hair, and stitched carefully along the wound.

She sat in the chair beside his bed, took his hand in hers, and began talking to him. Keren wasn't sure if he could hear her or even sense her presence, but she believed that her nightly prayers, whispered before sleep, might somehow make a difference. One day, she hoped, he would wake up.

She told him about her new job and reminisced about the moments they had shared before the accident. But Hezi lay there motionless, eyes closed, as if frozen in time. Keren eventually fell silent. She continued to hold his hand, staring at him for what felt like an eternity, wondering if he would ever recover—and if he did, what price she would have to pay. But she wasn't ready to give up hope.

Yulia suddenly entered the room. "You'll need to wrap up your visit," she said before stepping back out.

Keren gave Hezi one last, compassionate look. She gently released his hand, rose from the chair, and left the room.

Shortly after, Dr. Snir entered to monitor Hezi's condition. He reviewed the medical chart while Yulia, who had returned, adjusted the pillow beneath Hezi's head. As she smoothed out the bedding, her attention was drawn to a slight movement.

"Look, his finger moved," she said, pointing to Hezi's pinky finger.

Dr. Snir leaned in, observing closely. "It looks like his nervous system is beginning to respond. That's a good sign."

He made a note in Hezi's chart and slid it back into place. Just as he turned to leave, Yulia spoke.

"Have you thought about what I said?"

"About going out?"

"Yes."

"This weekend works for me," he replied with a brief smile before hurrying out of the room.

That evening, for the first time in a while, Keren sat with her parents to watch TV.

Her parents saw this as a positive sign. Until now, she had kept to herself, spending most of her time isolated in her room.

The news broadcast began with an unusual report:

In the Chinese city of Wuhan, a man had eaten a bat at a restaurant and contracted a strange, highly dangerous virus. The virus had already begun spreading across China. A doctor who identified the virus early and tried to raise the alarm had been silenced by the authorities. Later, he died under mysterious circumstances.

Keren thought the news report was entirely irrelevant. What does this have to do with us here in Israel? she wondered. There were far more important issues to cover—security, social problems, the economy...

"Did you visit Hezi today?" her mother suddenly asked.

"Yes."

"And how is he?"

"No change."

Her mother sighed. "I know you love him, but it's hard for me to believe he'll come out of this..." she repeated for the umpteenth time.

Keren cut her off, her frustration boiling over. "You're probably about to tell me to move on with my life. I'm tired of hearing it." She got up from her chair and stormed back to her room.

"You need to stop," Yotam said quietly to their mother.

"What did I even say?" Sarit asked, defensive.

"Just stop, that's all."

In her room, Keren sat at her desk and picked up a photograph of her and Hezi, taken during happier times. She cradled it in her hands, making a silent promise never to leave him, no matter how long it took. Even if it meant years of exhausting waiting, she believed—deep in her heart—that he would recover. The odds might seem slim now, but she refused to give up hope that they would one day be reunited, joyful and whole.

She opened a drawer, took out a small Book of Psalms, and softly recited a few chapters. When she finished, she tucked it back into the drawer and lay down to sleep.

But sleep didn't come easily. The nightmares persisted, merciless as ever. She woke in a panic, her forehead damp with sweat. The dark room felt suffocating as she tried to calm herself, her breath shallow. Every time she closed her eyes, the same terrifying dream returned—the terrorists from the restaurant, firing indiscriminately and murdering innocent people. They appeared more vivid than ever, dressed in black suits, their faces grim and unfeeling. In her dreams, they sowed chaos, destruction, and fear, chasing her relentlessly, threatening her existence in every horrifying way imaginable.

After what felt like an eternity, Keren finally managed to push the fear aside. Her body gave in to exhaustion, and she drifted back to sleep, worn out from the emotional battle.

Chapter 7

How many times have you met someone who claimed their life was perfect? That everything was exactly as they dreamed, with nothing they wanted to change or add? This was the kind of life Hezi had always dreamed of. He felt lucky to have such goodness. He lived in an old, modest apartment on the outskirts of the city—not wealthy, but content with little. For him, life was a gift made of small pleasures, simple experiences, and kind gestures.

And yet, this perfection felt strange to him, in ways he couldn't quite define. Over time, little changes began to creep in— details that might have seemed trivial to others, but to Hezi, they felt strange and unsettling. Keren came to visit Hezi

One evening, Hezi came home in high spirits. Keren was waiting at the door, greeting him with open arms.

"How was work, my love?" she asked with a warm smile, kissing him gently.

"It was great. I got recognized for the project I just finished—and a raise."

"Wonderful! There's no one like my husband." She beamed and took his hand. "I made you dinner. You must be starving."

A beautifully arranged meal awaited him in the kitchen, pleasing to both the eye and the appetite. Hezi sat down and began eating, but strangely, the food had no taste. Still, hunger drove him to continue eating. When he finished, a sense of regret washed over him—Why did I eat tasteless food? —but he didn't want to say anything to Keren and hurt her feelings.

"How was the food?" she asked.

"It was delicious," he lied.

Their two children came running to share stories from their day at school, but Keren gently signaled them away.

"Let Daddy rest. He's tired," she said.

Then she turned back to Hezi with a playful smile. "How about we take a dip in the lake? Just the two of us?"

"And the kids?"

"They'll only get in the way," she teased, her eyes twinkling.

"Alright," he agreed with a grin.

When they arrived at the lake, Hezi stood with Keren, gazing at the clear, blue water framed by green mountains. Near the shore was an old, abandoned dock. Other than an elderly man fishing from a small, weather-beaten boat in the middle of the lake, the place was empty.

Hezi undressed and entered the water naked, oddly not feeling the warmth of it. He called for Keren to join him. Keren undressed and entered the water as well.

When they reached the deeper water, they glanced toward the shore and, to their dismay, saw that more people had arrived at the lake. Leaving the water naked would now be tricky. But at that moment, it didn't bother them much. They clung to each other, hugging. Hezi kissed her softly on the lips. Then they splashed water at each other, dunking their heads under in a burst of laughter and joy.

Suddenly, the people disappeared. The sky darkened, and it began to rain—but Hezi didn't feel the rain. He dunked his head underwater, and when he surfaced, Keren was gone. He looked around, but she had vanished. He was alone. The lake turned stormy, the waves rising higher and higher. How could this be? he wondered. Hezi tried with all his might to reach the shore but couldn't. He screamed for help, but no one heard him.

The weather shifted just as suddenly as it had changed. The sky cleared, and the water calmed. It was strange. Hezi hurried to get out of the water, and when he looked down, he noticed he was fully clothed. How could this be?

He rushed back home, but when he arrived, he saw that the house's façade had changed. Wild bushes grew at the entrance, the gate was torn from its place, and the windows were painted a faded blue.

When he reached the door, it was locked, to his disappointment. He knocked hard, and a strange woman answered.

"Where's Keren?" he asked in fear, trying to push his way inside.

"Who is Keren?" she asked, blocking his way.

Hezi pushed past her and entered. The house was different from what he remembered. He walked down a hallway, searching for his children and wife, but there was no trace of them. The hallway stretched on, longer than before, with more rooms than he recalled. Strange and unsettling figures emerged from the rooms, glaring at him with anger for disturbing their peace. Fear gripped him as he considered turning back, but they surrounded him. He pushed them away, and they laughed, mocking him.

Hezi reached the living room, but the exit door was gone. Desperately, he looked for a window, but it was locked. He tried to open it, hoping to escape, but it wouldn't budge. He retreated into one of the dark rooms, shutting the door behind him to hide. He lay on a bed in the corner, expecting the worst.

Suddenly, he thought that perhaps this was all just a nightmare. He tried with all his might to wake up, shaking his head and shouting, "Enough!" But nothing happened. When he opened his eyes again, there was complete darkness around him. The figures had disappeared, and the house had transformed once more, becoming unrecognizable. The furniture was gone, replaced by a lone armchair, and on the white walls hung a faded landscape painting. He found himself lying in a large bed, and the only window was covered with a floral purple curtain. Indistinct voices and background noises drifted through the air.

Hezi didn't know where he was. He tried to get up from the bed but couldn't—his body was paralyzed. He tried to call for help, but no sound came from his throat. Helpless, he wondered if he was still dreaming. He didn't want to endure another strange, terrifying dream. Exhausted, he closed his eyes and sank into a deep sleep.

Hezi returned home, just as he did every day, happy and in good spirits. His wife, Keren, was waiting for him at the door, welcoming him with open arms.

"How was work, my dear?" she asked, smiling and kissing his lips softly.

"It was great. I received recognition for the project I just completed—and a raise," he replied.

"Wonderful. There's no one like my husband. I made you something to eat; you must be hungry," she said, taking his hand and leading him to the kitchen.

Hezi saw a beautifully set table before him, a feast for the eyes and the palate. He sat down and started thinking, this seems familiar. He knew exactly what would happen next. Here it comes. His wife approached him, about to ask if the food was good. He knew his children would soon appear, and she'd ask them not to disturb their father. Then it struck him—he might be dreaming again, stuck in a loop.

Unexpectedly, Hezi said, "You're not really here. None of this is real, is it?" But Keren remained silent. She didn't answer. The scenery around him began to change. The food on the table vanished. His wife disappeared. The door stood open, and strangers entered his house, wandering freely and eyeing him curiously. The furniture shifted, the balcony disappeared, replaced by a barred window.

Panicked, Hezi left his house. The car that had been parked outside was gone. In its place was a ground paved with cracked stones, with thorny wild bushes growing alongside. Across the way were ruined, neglected buildings. People whispered around him, and he looked terrified. He wanted to run for his life, but his legs wouldn't move. He closed his eyes, shook his head, and shouted, "Enough!"

When he opened his eyes, he was blinded by a bright light. He found himself lying in a bed once again, this time hooked up to IVs. Hezi tried to get up, but his body was still paralyzed. Yulia entered the room, checking on him. She gasped, shocked to find his eyes open, but he said nothing, a single tear rolling down his cheek. She ran out, calling for Dr. Snir.

Dr. Snir rushed in, excited.

"Do you know where you are?" he asked, curious.

"No."

"You're in a hospital. You suffered a severe head injury."

"Do you know your name?"

"I don't."

"Your name is Hezi," the doctor smiled.

Dr. Snir checked his pulse and temperature.

"Seems normal," he said to Yulia.

"Do you think he'll recover?" she asked.

"It's a slim chance. But who knows—miracles happen," Dr. Snir replied and left the room. Yulia followed, leaving Hezi alone.

Hezi fought with all his might not to fall asleep, dreading another return to that cursed dream. But exhaustion overwhelmed him, and soon, he drifted off again.

Chapter 8

Keren sat with her parents in the evening, watching the news. She sipped the instant coffee she had made earlier, her attention glued to the broadcast. The news opened with alarming developments from China. The government had begun setting up barriers throughout the country, and aerial footage showed a sprawling makeshift hospital compound filled with white tents. Doctors and nurses, their faces hidden behind masks, rushed around in protective suits.

The World Health Organization warned that the epidemic could spread beyond China's borders, potentially causing millions of deaths. Nations were urged to prepare for an emergency.

Keren shook her head, dismissing the report as exaggerated fearmongering. China is so far away—how could this affect us? she thought. The possibility of the virus reaching her life seemed remote at best.

Just then, her phone rang. She answered without checking the screen.

"Hello, this is Dr. Snir from the hospital. I wanted to let you know—Hezi has woken up."

The cup slipped from Keren's hand, crashing to the floor and shattering into pieces. Coffee spilled in all directions.

Her parents turned to her, startled.

"How is he?" Keren asked, her voice trembling.

"He's awake but mostly confused," Dr. Snir replied.

"Thank you—thank you so much. This is the best news," she said, ending the call.

Sarit's eyes widened. "What happened?"

"Hezi regained consciousness," Keren said, still in shock.

"That's wonderful!" Sarit exclaimed, though a flicker of concern crossed her face. She knew a long and difficult rehabilitation lay ahead, and even then, there were no guarantees Hezi would return to who he once was.

Sarit quickly fetched a mop and bucket, her excitement evident as she wiped up the spilled coffee and gathered the broken glass.

The following afternoon, Keren arrived at the hospital, her heart racing with anticipation. She hurried into Hezi's room, her eyes lighting up the moment she saw him awake in bed.

"Hezi, do you recognize me? It's me—Keren," she said, smiling warmly.

Hezi blinked, studying her for a moment. "Keren?" he repeated, his tone uncertain.

"Yes, it's me," she said, her heart lifting.

But Hezi shook his head, confusion clouding his face. "I have no idea who you are."

Keren's smile faltered. She hadn't expected this.

"You don't recognize me?" she asked, her voice laced with disbelief.

"No," he said flatly.

Yulia entered the room to perform a routine check.

"He doesn't recognize me," Keren whispered, her worry spilling over.

"Give him time," Yulia replied gently. "He's still confused." Yet, beneath her calm demeanor, Yulia knew there was a chance Hezi might never fully regain his memory. It was possible that parts of his brain had been permanently affected.

Keren tried to revive fragments of their past without mentioning anything tied to the trauma. But Hezi remained quiet, listening without much response, his gaze distant.

"Don't push him too hard," Yulia advised. "He needs space and time to recover."

With a reassuring smile, Yulia left the room, leaving Keren to sit quietly by Hezi's side, holding on to hope.

***

Three months had passed since Hezi was hospitalized, and his condition had steadily improved.

A woman approached his bedside, smiling warmly. "My name is Iris, and I'm your physical therapist," she introduced herself. She began the session by carefully moving his arms and legs, guiding his body through medical exercises. Afterward, she gave him a gentle massage.

Hezi winced as sharp pain shot through his left leg, which refused to cooperate. The frustration etched across his face was unmistakable.

"It'll take time for your leg to function properly," Iris said, offering reassurance. "But you're already looking much better."

"I'm afraid I'll be disabled for life," Hezi admitted, his voice filled with uncertainty.

"I believe everything will be okay," she responded confidently and continued her work.

After a while, she concluded the session. "That's it for today. Remember to move your body occasionally so it doesn't atrophy," she said with a friendly smile and left the room.

As Iris exited, Dr. Snir stepped inside for his routine check-up.

"Doctor, how am I doing?" Hezi asked eagerly.

"You're making excellent progress. Honestly, you're a bit of a medical miracle," Dr. Snir replied. "In all my years as a doctor, I've never seen someone arrive in intensive care with a gunshot wound to the head, given almost no chance of survival, and recover so quickly."

He paused, studying Hezi's face. "But you're still struggling with memory—forgetting people, events, and even small details. That's concerning. Let's hope it won't last too long."

"I just need to stay positive, right?" Hezi asked with a faint smile.

"Exactly," Dr. Snir replied warmly and made his way out of the room.

In the corridor, Dr. Snir ran into Yulia.

"Do you want to meet tonight?" she asked casually.

"What do you have in mind?"

"A romantic dinner by candlelight."

"Sounds good. Let's talk later—I need to run," he said with a grin before heading down the hallway toward the conference room.

Inside the conference room, Professor Levin addressed him as the final attendee entered.

"How is your patient, Hezi?" the professor inquired.

"He's still confused, has trouble recalling names, and finds it difficult to stay focused. His left leg isn't functioning well either," Dr. Snir reported.

Professor Levin sighed. "It's possible Hezi may stay in this state permanently. The fact that he's even alive is already a miracle."

"He has a strong will to recover," Dr. Snir replied, hopeful. "I believe he'll make a full recovery."

"That's good to hear. Have you heard about the mysterious epidemic spreading in China? They're calling it Corona."

Some of the attendees looked surprised, clearly hearing about it for the first time.

"There's already been a case reported outside China," Levin continued. "It happened in Ischgl, Austria, a popular ski resort. But don't worry—it's just one isolated case."

"An isolated case that spiraled out of control," Dr. Snir muttered under his breath.

"The Europeans know how to handle these situations. Trust them," Levin said confidently.

Still, Dr. Snir silently hoped the epidemic wouldn't reach Israel.

The meeting adjourned, and the doctors returned to their posts.

***

Keren arrived at the hospital for her usual visit. She found Hezi sitting on the bed with a nurse, practicing memory games. He was trying to match two cards with the same shape, struggling to remember where the matching card was. His frustration was clear.

57

"That's okay. You'll do better next time," the nurse said gently, gathering the cards before leaving the room.

Keren sat down in the chair beside the bed and smiled warmly at him.

"How are you feeling?" she asked softly.

Hezi focused his gaze on her, a flicker of confusion in his eyes.

"Remind me, who are you?" he asked helplessly.

"I'm your girlfriend, Keren."

"I have a girlfriend?"

"Yes, you do."

"I'm sorry, but I don't remember."

"That's okay. You'll remember," she assured him. "How are you feeling?"

"My leg hurts a lot. It's hard to move it."

"It'll pass. You'll get better—I'm sure of it."

"Do you remember why you ended up here?"

"No. It's like there's a black hole in my memory. I don't remember anything."

"That's normal," Keren explained gently. "Sometimes the brain suppresses difficult memories to help with healing and moving on."

"What bad things?" Hezi asked, curious.

"Nothing you need to worry about right now," she said with a restrained smile.

She reached into her bag, pulling out a chocolate bar and a bag of cookies.

"I brought you some sweets."

"Thank you. That's very kind of you," he said, accepting the treats.

Keren began talking about her new job and the interesting projects she was working on, but Hezi's interest seemed distant. He wanted to connect with her, but the blankness in his memory left him grasping for words.

A long silence settled between them. Keren watched him with quiet compassion as Hezi unwrapped the chocolate bar. He glanced at her and held out a piece.

"No thanks, I brought it for you," she said warmly, gesturing for him to eat it himself.

When he finished, he asked, "Do you come here often?"

"I try to, as long as I can," she replied with a soft smile.

"Tell me about the time we were together?"

"I'll tell you," Keren said playfully, "but only if you promise to make an effort to remember me next time I visit."

"I'll write your name on a note and won't forget you," he promised sincerely.

"Okay," Keren agreed, then told him about their first meeting. When she finished, she glanced at the clock. "I need to go now," she said gently.

Hezi wanted her to stay longer, but fatigue was beginning to weigh on him.

"The next time I come, I'd love to see some progress in your condition," she said hopefully.

Hezi looked at her silently, aware that even the smallest step forward would require immense effort. How could he promise her he would succeed in remembering?

"Remind me of your name again?" he asked softly.

"Keren," she said with a smile, leaning in to kiss his cheek.

She said goodbye and walked away, leaving Hezi behind with the warmth of her touch lingering.

Chapter 9

For the first time since being hospitalized, Hezi attempted to walk on his own. His left leg still hurt, and he had to use a walker, taking slow, deliberate steps while Nurse Sima watched over him. Hezi didn't get far. After a few steps, he was exhausted and wanted to sit down to rest. The effort he put into each step drained his energy. Finally, he gave up, returned to his room, and lay down on the bed, breathing heavily.

Later that afternoon, he sat again to play a memory game with the nurse, but once again, he lost, looking more frustrated than ever. "I can't remember the cards," he told her in despair.

"It's okay, next time," she replied, then got up and went on her way.

The days passed slowly without any significant news, except that his left leg had stopped hurting and was functioning normally again. Hezi got out of bed on his own, grabbed the pole with wheels on which the IV bag hung, and began to wander around the ward, looking with great curiosity. Eventually, he reached the reception desk and started asking the clerks a flurry of questions: Where am I? Who am I? When will I go home? How long have I been here?

Although the clerks were busy, they tried to take a moment now and then to answer him patiently. After getting some answers, he continued to explore the hospital corridors without interference. To his delight, he discovered a playroom and went inside. He sat on one of the chairs and examined the game displayed on the screen, but he quickly lost interest and returned outside. When he tried to go back to his room, he forgot the way and stood there, staring around helplessly.

"Are you lost?" Yulia remarked as she passed by and noticed him standing in the corridor, looking confused.

"Who are you?" he asked, surprised.

"I'm Nurse Yulia. And you are?" she inquired, hoping to see some improvement in his memory.

"I don't remember."

"Come, I'll take you to your room," she said, guiding him back. When they arrived, he thanked her and lay down on the bed, staring at the ceiling in frustration.

Keren came for one of her many visits, bringing photos from the time they were together before the incident. She entered the room where Hezi was hospitalized and sat down on the chair beside him. "I brought you a surprise," she said, taking an envelope out of her bag. Keren got up from the chair, sat on his bed, and showed him the pictures. "See, this is the photo of us at the beach together. Remember?" Hezi shook his head no. "And this is the picture of us sitting on the couch at my place. Remember?" Again, Hezi shook his head no. Keren pulled out photo after photo, and Hezi kept shaking his head. Finally, she put the pictures back in the envelope, looking frustrated.

"I'm sorry," he said, placing his hand on hers. "I wish I could remember; it's hard for me too. Sometimes I feel like a lost person wandering in a maze, trying to find my way out helplessly. Do you understand?" Keren smiled at him, gave him a small kiss on the forehead, and said, "Despite everything, I love you and believe that one day you'll remember me."

The visit ended, and Keren was about to leave when suddenly, Hezi grabbed her hand. "Thank you for supporting me; without you, I'd be lost." Hezi looked serious as he let go of her hand. Keren smiled and left the room. Although she didn't achieve her goal, she still saw it as progress.

***

Yulia wanted to travel to Europe and bought tickets for herself and Dr. Snir. The perfect destination was Rome, Italy. They planned to fly there for a week in the summer and eagerly awaited it. However,

Dr. Snir hurried to the ward, more worried than ever, approached Yulia, and said, "We need to talk; come with me to the office."

When they got to the office, he closed the door behind him and said, "We have to cancel the trip."

"Why? I've already paid," she said, surprised.

"Haven't you heard about the epidemic spreading across Europe, the Corona epidemic? The government is considering closing the airport."

Yulia looked disappointed. She had eagerly anticipated this vacation, and now the dream was shattered. "Won't this epidemic pass by summer? Maybe it's worth waiting and seeing instead of canceling the tickets and losing a lot of money."

Dr. Snir remained silent, realizing there was merit in her words. "Okay, let's get back to the ward before they notice we're gone."

***

Hezi's condition gradually improved. Nurse Smadar removed the bandage covering his head, following the doctor's orders. The marks from the surgery had already started to heal amid the hair that was beginning to grow back. Hezi walked independently through the ward's corridors and was sometimes seen chatting with the nurses at the reception desk. In his free time, he watched TV in the reception area and occasionally played on the computer in the playroom. The doctors predicted that in two weeks at most, he could return home.

                                    ***

Keren came to visit Hezi, as usual, and found him joking with his doctor, Dr. Snir. She entered the room and sat down on the chair.

"I see you're already healthy," she remarked.

"Who is she?" Hezi asked Dr. Snir.

"I think you already know," Dr. Snir replied with a smile, then left the room.

"Why does he say I know?" Hezi asked aloud, his voice filled with confusion.

"Because it's time for you to know. I come here many times to visit you, and you still don't recognize me?" Keren said, her tone soft but tinged with sadness.

"What can I do? I don't remember," Hezi replied helplessly.

Keren tried to hide her worry, but it lingered. Hezi would be discharged soon, yet he still didn't remember anything. He wouldn't be able to live on his own, let alone take care of himself, and Keren feared he would become a burden on those around him. If his memory didn't return soon, she might have to leave her job and move in to care for him. And who knew how long that would last?

"I brought you a memory game. You'll like it," she said, pulling a deck of cards from her bag.

She spread the cards on the bed and explained the rules—he had to draw two cards at a time and try to remember them. The goal was to match cards with identical shapes and colors. Hezi tried, concentrating hard, but each attempt ended in failure.

"I'm sorry, it's not working," he muttered, frustrated.

"It's okay, next time," Keren reassured him, gathering the cards and slipping them back into her bag.

She started talking about her job, hobbies, family, and their time together before the accident—stories she had told him countless times before. Hezi mostly listened, offering little response. As the visiting hour drew to a close and Keren prepared to leave, Hezi suddenly spoke.

"Keren, will you come to visit me tomorrow?"

"What did you call me?" she asked, taken aback.

"Keren. You're my girlfriend, right?"

Keren looked at him skeptically. Just because he remembered her name didn't mean he truly knew who she was.

"What do you really remember about me?" she pressed.

"I remember you always said that patience is the fastest way."

Keren smiled, her heart lightening.

"That's right. I used to say that when you wanted things to happen right away."

"It looks like you're starting to remember," she said, excitement flickering in her voice. "That's a good sign."

"I guess it is," Hezi replied softly.

"Well, I have to go."

"Okay, goodbye," Hezi said, waving at her.

***

A week later, Dr. Snir called Keren in the evening and said, "Hezi is healthy and ready to go home."

"Great! I'll come to get him tomorrow," she replied, then added, "And what about his memory?"

"I believe you'll start seeing improvement soon," he assured her.

Keren was thrilled but uncertain. She wasn't sure Hezi was ready to live alone just yet, so she decided to move in with him until his memory improved, and he could manage on his own—maybe even return to work.

The next morning, Keren arrived at the hospital in high spirits. Dr. Snir met her at the reception desk.

"The discharge papers are ready," he said, handing them to her.

"Thank you for everything, Doctor," Keren said warmly.

"It's my job," he replied with a smile and hurried off to another patient's room.

Keren continued down the corridor to Hezi's room and found him sitting on the bed, already dressed and ready to leave.

"How are you feeling?" she asked with a bright smile.

"Better than ever," Hezi answered.

"Great. I'm here to take you home."

"I'm ready," he said, standing up eagerly.

As they made their way out, Hezi stopped to say goodbye to the medical staff, thanking them for their dedicated care.

"I'll never forget everything you've done for me," he told them sincerely.

Chapter 10

For the first time in a long while, Hezi walked into his home, taking slow, measured steps as he absorbed his surroundings. The house looked exactly as he had left it, only now it appeared tidier and cleaner.

"The house looks neat," he remarked.

"Do you like it?" Keren asked.

"Yes, thank you for everything."

Keren smiled. "Go take a shower and change your clothes. I'll make us some dinner—you must be hungry."

"Okay," he said, heading to the bathroom as she suggested.

When Hezi returned to the living room after his shower, he looked clean and refreshed. On the dining table, dinner was already set: an omelet, fresh salad, cheese spread, bread, and orange juice.

"This looks delicious," he said as he sat down to eat.

"Thank you," Keren replied with a smile, joining him at the table.

After dinner, they moved to the living room to watch the evening news. A young announcer, wearing a serious expression, began the broadcast with a startling announcement:

"The coronavirus pandemic has spread worldwide. In response, the Prime Minister has taken the unprecedented step of imposing a nationwide lockdown. The skies are closed—no flights in or out. All non-essential businesses and factories will shut down, cultural events are canceled, and restaurants and event halls will close immediately. Leaving the house is prohibited, except for emergencies or to buy food and medicine."

The broadcast shifted to a panel of health experts, who launched into a heated debate. Some supported the lockdown, while others opposed it, with a few even suggesting it was part of a government conspiracy.

Hezi groaned and asked Keren to turn off the television.

"My head hurts from all this noise," he said. "I just want some peace—to sort my thoughts and process everything. More information will only make it harder."

"Would you like me to make you some coffee?" Keren offered.

"No, I think I just want to sleep," Hezi replied, standing up from the couch.

He headed to the bedroom to get ready for bed. Keren stayed behind in the living room, lost in her thoughts. This time, her worry wasn't just about Hezi's recovery but about the uncertainty of her own future. What if she lost her job? How would she manage? Without an income, paying bills would become a struggle, and buying food would be a challenge. The problems felt overwhelming—Hezi's delicate condition was only beginning to improve, and now this mysterious pandemic threatened to upend everything.

Early the next morning, the phone rang, jolting Keren awake and bringing her worst fears to life. It was her employer, Maya.

"I'm so sorry, Keren," Maya said in a strained voice. "I have to put you on unpaid leave. Let's hope it's only temporary."

Keren tried to reason with Maya, explaining how complicated her life had become with Hezi's recovery. But Maya was struggling too.

"I understand," Maya said gently. "But I had to shut down the business I've worked so hard to build. I might lose clients, and I'm not even sure the business will survive."

Keren didn't know what else to say. The conversation ended with a faint, "When things get better, I'll bring you back. I promise."

But when would things get better? How long would it take? There were only questions—no answers.

On Monday morning, the chaos reached new heights. Crowds stormed the grocery stores, emptying shelves. Keren went to the neighborhood supermarket, only to be greeted by long lines that snaked through the aisles. A young employee stood at the entrance, trying in vain to maintain order as people pushed forward, terrified that essential items—like eggs and toilet paper—would soon be gone.

When Keren finally made it inside, she found that many of the shelves had already been cleared. Eggs, along with most canned goods, were nowhere to be found. Panic-buying was in full swing as people hoarded food and prepared for the worst.

Despite the shortages, Keren managed to gather some basic groceries and returned to Hezi's home.

***

A week passed, and the scale of the disaster only worsened. News broadcasts opened with harrowing images from Italy. Hundreds of people were dying every day. Military trucks rolled through streets, transporting coffins, and when cemeteries ran out of space, mass burials began.

Hospitals looked like warzones. Doctors and nurses, dressed in full-body white suits and masks, spoke in broken voices about the collapse of the healthcare system and the desperate shortage of ventilators. A nurse, visibly shaken and on the verge of tears, described the heart-wrenching scenes she had witnessed—patients slipping away before her eyes, powerless to save them.

Hezi stared at the television, horrified. "What should we do?" he asked Keren, his voice heavy with fear.

"We just need to follow the health ministry's guidelines and stay at home. Everything will be okay," she replied, trying to sound reassuring. But her words offered little comfort—not to Hezi, and not even to herself. She was scared of the unknown, frightened that the situation would drag on, bringing more devastation closer to home.

Keren's thoughts drifted to her job. She no longer believed her employer would call her back, and the possibility of finding new work seemed slim. The uncertainty gnawed at her—how would she manage without an income?

New restrictions rolled in daily, fueling her unease. "Don't touch door handles. Avoid elevators. Don't sneeze in public. No handshakes." Each announcement was another weight on her mind, making the future feel more uncertain and harder to bear.

***

Passover arrived, and the streets were deserted—no one coming or going, as if time itself had frozen. Fear of the unknown gripped the city, and residents remained behind closed doors, dreading what might come next.

Keren and Hezi sat at the table, which was filled with an abundance of food, but the air felt heavy with loneliness. A holiday typically marked by large family gatherings, reading the Haggadah, singing, laughing, and enjoying festive meals, now felt somber and muted.

At midnight, people began stepping onto their balconies, singing and clapping in an attempt to stave off the isolation. Curious, Keren and Hezi joined them on their balcony. For a brief moment, it seemed as if the lifeless streets were coming back to life, filled with voices and presence. But after about an hour, the residents retreated indoors, and the oppressive silence returned.

"Let's go to bed; it's already late," Keren suggested softly.

Hezi sat in discomfort, feeling suffocated. The days of confinement—first in the hospital, now at home—were weighing on him. He longed to step outside, breathe fresh air, and change his surroundings. He craved conversation, connection, and normalcy, but none of that was possible.

"Okay," he mumbled reluctantly, rising from the chair and heading to bed.

As the lights went out, darkness and silence settled in once again. Thoughts and worries swirled in their minds, growing heavier with each passing moment, threatening to steal their sleep.

Chapter 11

The passing days did little to ease the couple's burden. Unable to work, they were forced to stay home, relying on meager unemployment benefits. Every evening, the television aired stories of people crying in despair after losing their jobs.

Confused parents struggled to navigate school schedules, trying to figure out which days their children should attend, with which group or "capsule," and at what time. The concept of the reproduction number—a metric for tracking the spread of the virus—became part of daily life. At first, the graphs showed a promising decline, prompting the government to lift the lockdown. But soon, a new outbreak spread rapidly, forcing the government to impose another lockdown.

Disruptions swept across the country. Young people defied restrictions, throwing large, maskless parties, leaving the police scrambling to maintain order and issuing fines to violators. In the ultra-Orthodox sector, large funerals continued to be held, with the police standing by helplessly. Meanwhile, mass weddings in Arab communities also became commonplace. For nearly a year, enforcement efforts struggled to curb the violations, and public patience wore thin.

Relief finally came with the announcement of a nationwide vaccination campaign, swiftly organized by the Ministry of Health. Long lines formed at vaccination centers as people eagerly received their first and second doses. Slowly, compliance improved, and violations began to dwindle.

Keren breathed a sigh of relief. The thought of shedding her mask and resuming normal life filled her with hope. She was ready to look for a new job, knowing there was no point in trying to return to her old one—someone else had already taken her place. She wasn't disappointed, though. Young, energetic, and with some experience under her belt, she was confident that new opportunities would come.

Her optimism, however, was clouded by concerns about Hezi. Though his physical recovery from the injury was remarkable, he struggled to reintegrate into everyday life. He often forgot small things—where he had left his phone or what he intended to do at a particular moment. Their relationship was a mix of frustrations and joys, with ups and downs, but Keren believed that in time, things would improve.

One morning, Keren shared a new idea with Hezi.

"I have a lead on a job, but I'll need to leave you alone for a few hours," she said.

"How will I manage alone? What if I need help?" he asked, anxiety creeping into his voice.

"You can always call me," she assured him, planting a soft kiss on his lips before leaving.

Hezi remained at home, staring at the closed door for what felt like forever, hoping Keren would return sooner than later. The empty house felt oppressive, the silence unsettling, and even the street outside seemed threatening. Panic flickered within him, but he forced himself to snap out of it. He made a cup of coffee and turned on the TV, deciding to distract himself with a comedy.

Around noon, Keren returned, and Hezi greeted her eagerly.

"How did the interview go?" he asked, curiosity lighting up his face.

"It went well. They said they'd get back to me in the next few days," she replied.

"I believe you'll get the job," he said with a smile.

Keren couldn't help but feel comforted by his encouragement. It's always nice to hear something positive during uncertain times, she thought.

"Did you do anything today?" she asked gently.

"No," Hezi admitted. "I just can't focus on anything."

"Maybe you could find a hobby—something to keep you busy and that you'd enjoy," Keren suggested.

Hezi fell silent. He was afraid of being a burden on Keren, and the idea of finding a new hobby felt daunting.

After a pause, he quietly said, "Sit down and rest. I'll make us lunch."

Keren smiled, pleased by his initiative, though she wasn't entirely confident the meal would turn out well. To her surprise—and delight—Hezi proved her wrong.

The next day, Hezi was left alone again as Keren went out for another job interview. She wanted to increase her chances of finding something that matched her skills.

Hezi wandered aimlessly around the house, feeling lost and uneasy. Fear began to creep in again, and he realized Keren was right—he needed to find something to occupy his time. Suddenly, an idea flashed through his mind: he would photograph people on the streets, especially those who had experienced life's hardships and bore the visible marks of time.

Hezi went to his room, retrieved an old camera from the closet, and left the house. He headed down to the bustling street, camera in hand. There were plenty of interesting people to photograph, but Hezi was searching for more than just a snapshot—he wanted to capture the perfect image. One that would intrigue, unsettle, and make the viewer pause, as if searching for something hidden within it.

The noisy street didn't feel right. He preferred a quieter space where moments of stillness could unfold naturally. He walked to a nearby park, found a bench, and sat down, gazing at the serene landscape. Birds flitted among the treetops, while stray cats leapt onto the benches, basking in the gentle sunlight. Now and then, passersby wandered by, heading toward unknown destinations, slowly fading into the distance.

Hezi sat for over an hour, waiting for the right moment, but nothing worthy of capturing revealed itself. Disappointed, he finally stood up and made his way back home.

By midday, Keren returned home to find lunch prepared and neatly set on the table.

"How was the interview?" Hezi asked, curiosity lighting up his tired face.

"I didn't get the job," Keren said, shrugging.

"Never mind," Hezi replied encouragingly. "You'll nail it next time."

"How was your day?" she asked, settling into her chair

"Boring," he admitted. "I didn't take a single picture."

Keren gave a small smile. "Well, there's another election next week—the fourth one in two years. You might catch some good shots—maybe even a fight or an argument between the different political camps."

"Do you think we'll finally get a resolution?" Hezi asked.

Keren sighed. "I've stopped caring. Whatever happens, we'll still be the ones paying for the government's dysfunction—no budget, a growing deficit, and higher taxes. It's just going to get harder."

"It'll only widen the gap between different parts of society," Hezi added thoughtfully.

"Exactly.

"It's a grim outlook," he said. "Let's eat before the food gets cold."

That night, Hezi was haunted once again by nightmares—visions of death, corpses, and cries of despair. He woke in a panic, heart pounding, beads of sweat forming on his brow. Staring into the darkness, he struggled to calm himself. When sleep wouldn't return, he got up, drank some cold water, and lay back down, exhausted.

Keren, too, sometimes had troubled dreams. At times, she would mumble unintelligible words in her sleep, but she always managed to shake them off and move on.

Eventually, Hezi drifted back to sleep. But this time, something different happened: a fleeting image appeared, only to vanish just as quickly.

In the dream, he saw a girl wearing a yellow skirt, her black hair braided into two pigtails. Her expression was blank, vacant. At first, Hezi dismissed the dream as meaningless. But the next day, while watching television, he saw the same girl's photo on the news.

The headline read: "Missing Girl with Intellectual Disabilities."

A chill ran down Hezi's spine. He decided not to tell Keren, afraid she would think he was imagining things—or worse, that he was losing his grip on reality.

***

Keren received the long-awaited phone call. On the line was Tzipora, the HR manager, informing her that she had been accepted for the job.

"When do you think you can start?" Tzipora asked.

"Tomorrow," Keren replied.

"Great. Come by at eight so we can fill out the paperwork and prepare your ID badge."

"Okay," Keren said, trying to keep her excitement in check.

She shared the news with Hezi, who immediately lit up.

"We should celebrate," he said. "How about pizza?"

"I was thinking more like a restaurant," Keren replied with a smile.

"A restaurant?" Hezi's excitement dimmed, replaced by growing anxiety. "I don't think that's a good idea."

"We need to overcome the fear. Only by going out and realizing it's not as bad as it seems will the fear start to go away."

"Easy for you to say. I'm the one who got shot, remember?"

"We'll go, and if at any point you feel overwhelmed, we can leave. Deal?"

Hezi hesitated, then nodded. "Okay."

At the restaurant, Hezi insisted on sitting by the window, scanning the other diners nervously. His gaze darted around the room, taking in every detail as though danger might appear at any moment.

"Shall we order something?" Keren suggested gently.

Hezi struggled to concentrate, and beads of sweat began to form on his forehead. Sensing his unease, Keren reached across the table and held his hand.

"Don't be afraid. You're not alone. We'll be okay."

Gradually, Hezi's breathing steadied. "I'll have coffee and cake," he said.

"Me too," Keren smiled, glad to see him relax a little.

The waitress arrived, took their order, and returned shortly with their coffee and cake.

"Thank you," Keren said as the waitress placed the tray on the table and left.

"You need to relax," she said softly.

"I'm trying," Hezi muttered, though the tension still clung to him like a second skin. He took small bites of cake and sipped his coffee, his eyes still flickering nervously around the room.

After a few moments, Hezi turned to Keren, his expression softening.

"On this occasion, I want to thank you for everything you've done for me. Without you, I would have sunk into a dark, paralyzed place. You gave me hope—and a reason to keep going."

Keren squeezed his hand. "You would've done the same for me," she said warmly.

Hezi smiled, but just then, something outside the window caught his eye. A shiver ran through him.

"It's her," he whispered, his voice tight with urgency.

"Who?" Keren asked, startled.

Hezi stood abruptly, pointing toward the street. "It's her."

Without another word, Hezi rushed out of the restaurant. Keren barely had time to react before he disappeared through the door.

"Hezi smiled. Suddenly, he noticed a figure passing by on the street near the window where he was sitting. Fear struck him, and a shiver ran down his spine as he quickly looked away.

"What happened?" Keren asked, concerned.

"It's her, it's her," he whispered, pointing to the window as he hastily got up from his seat.

Keren didn't have time to respond or ask who he meant before Hezi rushed out of the restaurant and ran outside.

"Hey," he called out to the figure, approaching slowly so as not to scare her.

The girl stopped and turned to face him.

"You don't know me, but I want to help," Hezi said gently. "I know you're lost—and probably hungry and thirsty. You don't have to be afraid. I'd like to invite you to eat with us."

The girl hesitated, eyeing him suspiciously.

"What's your name?" Hezi asked softly.

"Shira," she replied.

"Shira. Your family is looking for you. They're very worried." He extended his hand. "Come with me. Let's get you something to eat."

After a moment's hesitation, Shira took his hand, and Hezi led her back to the restaurant.

When they reached the table, Hezi introduced her.

"This is Shira—the girl who went missing. Order her some food. I'll call the police."

Keren nodded and gently helped Shira settle into a seat. She made sure Shira felt safe while they waited for the police to arrive.

About half an hour later, two officers entered the restaurant, took Hezi's statement, and escorted Shira away.

Hezi sat back down, picking up his coffee as if nothing unusual had happened. Keren stared at him, stunned.

"How did you know it was her?" she finally asked.

"I saw her picture on TV," Hezi said simply.

That evening, after the lights went out, Keren reached across the bed and stroked Hezi's head.

"I'm proud of you," she whispered, pressing a soft kiss to his lips. "You made it through the day."

"It's all thanks to you," Hezi murmured.

"I love you," Keren said, her voice barely above a whisper.

"I love you too," he replied.

Keren's hand drifted from his head to his chest, and she kissed him again. Her touch grew more intimate, exploring his body until it reached his groin. Hezi's body responded, warmth spreading through him as he felt himself harden beneath her hand.

"We should undress," she whispered in his ear.

Hezi's heart raced as he followed her lead, quickly shedding his clothes. He watched, mesmerized, as Keren undressed slowly, her movements graceful and deliberate. She lay back on the bed, her bare skin glowing softly in the moonlight that filtered through the blinds.

Hezi moved closer, kissing her deeply. His hands traced over her body, lingering on her breasts before traveling down to her belly and further south.

They made love, their bodies moving in unison—back and forth, like waves rising and falling with the tide. Their sweat mingled as they became one, losing themselves in each other's touch. For a moment, all their fears, anxieties, and loneliness melted away, dissolving into the night.

They kissed and caressed, savoring each other's presence as the pale moonlight cast strange, flickering shadows on the walls.

Chapter 12

Election day arrived faster than expected. Hezi left home with his camera slung over his shoulder, accompanied by Keren, determined to capture the perfect shot that would encapsulate the day's atmosphere. However, upon arriving at the polling station, he found the mood disappointingly lethargic. Campaign workers slouched in plastic chairs, uninterested in persuading passersby to vote for their parties.

A young woman approached, offering him a voting slip. Hezi gave a polite but firm gesture, signaling that he wasn't interested.

Keren entered the school building where the elections were taking place, while Hezi stayed outside, as cameras weren't allowed inside. He positioned himself in the middle of the square, scanning the scene in search of something worth photographing—but nothing caught his eye.

Before long, Keren reappeared and walked toward him.

"Did you find anything interesting?" she asked.

"No," he answered, disappointment evident in his voice.

He handed her the camera and went inside to cast his vote. While waiting, Keren seized the opportunity to snap a few shots of two political activists loudly arguing. Although the confrontation was heated, it stopped short of turning physical.

When Hezi returned, Keren handed the camera back with a playful smile.

"I took a few pictures," she said.

Hezi grinned faintly as they began the walk home. He hadn't captured the shot he was hoping for, but he still held out hope that someday he would.

As soon as they got home, Hezi sat down and spoke with Keren.

"I've been thinking. I want to find a job," he said. "I need to get back into the workforce, even if it's part-time. Staying at home all day isn't good for me. I'm getting bored."

Keren nodded thoughtfully. "You can't jump straight back into high-tech, though. It's too demanding—long hours, constant pressure. I don't think it's the right thing for you right now."

"No, not high-tech," Hezi agreed. "Something else. Something flexible, with reasonable hours. I just need to do something."

One night, Hezi woke up in a panic, cold sweat dampening his forehead. In his dream, he witnessed a fatal car accident. A woman was crossing the street while the pedestrian light was green when a black car struck her with brutal force, throwing her far across the pavement. The driver didn't stop, fleeing the scene without hesitation. Hezi recognized the intersection—it was near his home.

Unable to sleep, he sat up in bed, his pulse racing. Keren lay beside him, curled up in a fetal position, fast asleep, unaware of his distress. He quietly slipped out of bed, drank a glass of cold water, and eventually returned to sleep, though his rest remained troubled.

The next morning, after Keren left for work, Hezi grabbed his camera and headed out. He had to see if the intersection from his dream held any clues or signs of danger. He found a spot nearby and sat down, carefully observing the surroundings. An hour passed, then two. Nothing happened.

Disappointed but relieved that the dream hadn't come true, Hezi made his way back home, a mixture of frustration and gratitude weighing on his mind. While no harm had come to anyone, he couldn't shake the feeling that he had wasted his morning chasing a phantom.

At the dining table, he opened his laptop and began searching for jobs. He wasn't sure what to focus on—he knew he wasn't ready to return to high-tech, and he didn't want anything physically demanding. The thought struck him: photography. Maybe he could work with media outlets or in journalism. After some searching, he found a few promising job listings and sent off his resume.

That afternoon, Keren returned home, exhausted. She tossed her bag aside and collapsed on the sofa, closing her eyes in search of a brief nap. Hezi had just finished preparing dinner and joined her on the couch.

"How was your day?" he asked.

"Tiring," she replied without opening her eyes.

"Go take a shower and get ready to eat," he suggested gently.

"We need to do some shopping," she mumbled. "I'll handle it later," he promised.

Keren slowly got up and shuffled to the bathroom for a shower.

Later that afternoon, Hezi headed out to the neighborhood supermarket. This time, he left his camera at home, carrying only a cloth bag for groceries. He planned to pick up just a few essentials.

On the way, he passed the intersection from his dream. He paused, scanning the street for any signs of danger. But there was nothing. "Just a foolish dream," he muttered to himself, brushing off the lingering unease.

The neighborhood supermarket was a meeting place between the neighbors who were shopping. The seller, Guy, greeted him warmly as always. Though the store didn't stock everything the larger supermarkets had; it carried the essentials Hezi needed. He filled his bag, paid, and started walking back home.

As he approached the intersection, a black car suddenly roared down the street. Before Hezi could react, the car struck a pedestrian with a sickening impact and sped off, leaving the victim crumpled on the asphalt.

Hezi froze in horror, clutching his head. His dream had come to life. For a moment, he was paralyzed by shock, but then instinct kicked in. He sprinted to the scene and called the police.

"Stay back!" Hezi shouted at the curious bystanders who began to gather around the injured woman.

She lay motionless, a pool of blood spreading beneath her. Her lifeless eyes stared into the sky.

Within minutes, the wail of sirens filled the air. An ambulance arrived, followed by a police car. Paramedics leaped from the ambulance, rushing a stretcher to the injured woman. They gently lifted her, connected her to a resuscitation device, and carried her into the ambulance.

Meanwhile, police officers began gathering witness statements. A stern-faced officer, Oren Levi, approached Hezi.

"Did you see what happened?" the officer asked.

"Yes," Hezi replied, still shaken. "A black Mazda hit her and kept going."

"Did you get a look at the driver?"

"A young man."

"Were you able to catch the license plate?"

"No," Hezi admitted regretfully.

Officer Levi noted the details as the ambulance sped away, sirens blaring. Hezi stood rooted to the spot, even after the officer moved on to interview other witnesses. The scene haunted him. He stared at the bloodstain on the road, unable to tear his eyes away.

After a long moment, he finally gathered himself, picked up his grocery bag, and walked home in a daze.

That night, Hezi struggled to fall asleep. The image of the woman's lifeless body, her vacant eyes, and the blood on the road played on an endless loop in his mind. Keren slept soundly beside him, blissfully unaware of the tragedy that had unfolded.

Hezi lay awake, tormented by the fear that Keren wouldn't understand—or worse, that she'd think he was losing his grip on reality. So, he kept the events of the day to himself, the weight of his silence pressing down like a heavy stone.

Chapter 13

In the following days, Hezi decided that before going to bed, he would watch funny movies to distract himself from thoughts of the tragic accident. He concluded that comedies helped him sleep better and enjoy more pleasant dreams.

One morning, he was surprised by a phone call. On the line was Gideon, the editor-in-chief of a well-known newspaper called News Today.

"My name is Gideon. I wanted to ask if you're still looking for a job?" he inquired.

"Yes, absolutely," Hezi replied.

"We're looking for a photographer for the crime section. Are you interested?"

"Yes, definitely."

"Come by tomorrow morning to the press building on Frishman Street, and we'll talk."

"Alright," Hezi said before hanging up. It struck him as odd that they hadn't asked about his work experience, which was usually a requirement.

Excitement bubbled within Hezi as he anticipated the meeting. Until that moment, he had never met field reporters, editors, or investigators face-to-face. It felt like stepping into a new and unfamiliar world. The thought of being part of the process of delivering news to the public was both thrilling and intriguing. When he shared the news with Keren after she returned from work, he was met with mixed emotions. On one hand, she was happy for him, glad that he had found such an interesting job; on the other hand, she expressed concern that the scenes he would encounter, especially those involving crime and violence, might prove too difficult for him to handle.

***

The building looked gray and outdated, situated in the heart of a busy main street. Hezi arrived, filled with excitement. The security guard at the entrance verified his personal details, checked that he wasn't carrying any weapons, and let him in.

Hezi stepped into the elevator, taking measured steps, and reached the second floor. When the elevator doors opened, he saw a large space filled with desks separated by partitions, with people sitting in front of computer screens. Some were talking to each other, while others were on the phone. The place buzzed like a beehive.

As Hezi stepped out of the elevator into the workspace, he encountered an employee passing by and asked where the editor-in-chief, Gideon Shechter, was sitting.

"He's over there, in the glass office," the employee pointed before continuing on his way.

Hezi approached the office entrance. "May I come in?" he asked politely.

Gideon shook his hand and invited him to sit down. He then signaled for Hezi to wait and called one of the journalists to join them. Shortly, she arrived at his office.

"Meet Tamar Friedman. She's a crime reporter—one of the best."

Hezi turned and saw her standing at the entrance. She looked attractive, dressed in tailored clothes that flattered her figure.

"From today, Hezi will be part of your team. Show him where the photography equipment is and give him a brief overview of your activities," Gideon instructed her.

With a grin, he added, "Be nice to him so he doesn't run away."

"Alright, I will," she replied reluctantly, turning to Hezi. "Follow me."

In the past, Tamar had not gotten along with the photographers who accompanied her, often scolding and reprimanding them. Some were offended and resigned, while others simply left without warning. She was tough and uncompromising, and some had called her various derogatory names before storming off in anger.

Tamar led Hezi to her desk. "Sit!" she ordered him. Hezi obediently complied.

Tamar opened her screen and showed him photos from various crime scenes.

"This is the level I expect from you. Do you think you can meet my demands?"

The different shooting angles and the use of natural light or camera flashes clearly indicated that these were taken by a professional photographer.

Hezi had no professional experience and knew he couldn't meet her expectations.

"Yes," he lied, hoping it wouldn't be discovered too soon, causing him to be fired on the spot.

"Good. In that case, come with me to the storage room, sign for the photography equipment, and in an hour, we'll head out to the field."

Hezi didn't expect to go out to the field so soon—especially not on his first day. Fear began to creep in, but he pulled himself together, went to the storage room, and returned with the photography equipment. He hoped to learn how to operate it quickly before Tamar lost her patience and fired him. While waiting for her, he attempted to use the advanced camera and was somewhat successful, though he wasn't familiar with all the shooting options, which would require time and experience.

Tamar was on her cell phone and ignored his presence. When she finished, she briefly told him, "Domestic violence. The husband killed his wife. Let's go."

Hezi loaded the photography equipment into the trunk, climbed into Tamar's car, and sat beside her. The car sped through the streets, bypassing traffic jams and red lights, driving downside roads and narrow lanes until they arrived at the scene. The police and rescue forces had already blocked access.

Hezi got out of the car, relieved to have arrived safely after the wild and dangerous drive. He managed to spot a woman's body being carried out of the house on a stretcher and took a few photos. He then noticed a man being led, handcuffed, to a police car and captured an image of him entering the vehicle.

"Come with me, and we'll interview one of the neighbors for more details," Tamar instructed him.

One of the neighbors said she heard shouting and threats through the door and decided to call the police. She explained that the door was locked, and no one could enter and intervene. She seemed agitated.

The police firmly asked all journalists, photographers, and onlookers to move away from the scene.

Tamar considered confronting the police, claiming that the public had a right to know, but she changed her mind.

"Did you get everything?" she asked.

"Yes."

"Good, let's go back."

The drive back was calmer, but Tamar remained mostly silent, as if lost in her own private world.

When they arrived, Hezi sat in Tamar's office, uploaded the photos to the computer, and reviewed them with her.

Finally, she said, "Good work, though there's room for improvement."

"Thanks," Hezi said, breathing a sigh of relief as he realized he had passed an important test.

"That's it for today. You can go. If something urgent comes up, I'll call you."

Hezi arrived home feeling happy and satisfied. Keren had been waiting anxiously for him.

"So, how was your first day at work?" she asked.

"Fascinating," he replied, detailing his experiences throughout the day.

"Was it difficult for you to see the scenes you encountered?" she asked.

"Not particularly," he answered briefly.

Hezi went into the shower to wash off the day's trials, closing his eyes and humming an old tune to himself.

Later in the evening, Hezi watched TV while Keren got ready for bed. When he climbed into bed, he found Keren sleeping with her back turned to him.

Hezi lay down beside her, the excitement from the day keeping him awake, and his sexual desire stirred. He touched her arm.

"I'm tired," she whispered.

Disappointed, Hezi lay on his back, trying to close his eyes but unable to do so.

He got up from the bed, went to the kitchen for a glass of water, returned to bed, and eventually fell asleep.

Chapter 14

The days passed in a blur. Hezi became skilled at photography. The scenes he captured varied, but they primarily focused on violence, murder, property destruction, arson, and theft. Under every article in the newspaper, there was a picture of the scene he had taken. Suspects were photographed from different angles—some with their faces uncovered, others wearing hats and masks that concealed their identities.

The collaboration between Tamar and Hezi grew stronger. Hezi arrived at work at unusual hours—sometimes early in the morning, sometimes in the middle of the night. There was never a dull moment; not a single day passed without a criminal event, sometimes even two in a day.

However, the sights he was exposed to began to weigh heavily on him. Hezi struggled to sleep at night, and when he sought attention, love, affection, or physical touch, he was met with a cold shoulder. Keren explained that dealing with clients who complained about the homes she designed for them left her frustrated, disappointed, and in a low mood. The work was exhausting her, and she was tired and wanted to sleep.

Hezi tried to understand her, but the moments of intimacy they had shared, especially at night in bed, significantly decreased, leaving him feeling frustrated and helpless. He hoped for better days in his relationship with Keren. There were moments when he considered quitting his job due to the harsh scenes and returning to a life of idleness, but he ultimately dismissed that possibility.

***

The nights became particularly long, and Hezi struggled to fall asleep. Many thoughts flooded his mind, threatening to drown him in a sea of impossible scenarios. Everything mixed together in his head, exhausting him like waves relentlessly crashing on a deserted shore. Finally, he fell asleep out of sheer exhaustion, and in his dream, he saw masses of people dressed in black, crowded and jostling their way through a narrow passage, stepping on and trampling each other, crying out for help, but there was no one to save them.

Hezi woke up in a panic. Keren continued to sleep deeply. As usual, he went to drink some water and returned to bed, but he couldn't fall back asleep and stayed awake for a long time.

In the morning, Hezi received an urgent phone call. It was Tamar, asking him to come to the newspaper building. "There's a new corruption case at Bat Yam's city hall," she said briefly. Hezi, who was very tired, gathered his remaining strength and went to work.

When he arrived, Tamar showed him a picture of the suspect. "He embezzled city funds," she stated emphatically.

Hezi quickly drank his morning coffee, hurried to grab his photography equipment, and got ready to move. Tamar was waiting for him in her car. Hezi loaded the equipment into the trunk and quickly sat beside her. On the way to the scene, he thought he heard an interesting news report on the radio. "Can you turn up the radio, please?"

Tamar complied, and the announcer said, "Thousands of people will gather tonight at Mount Meron to celebrate the revelry of Rabbi Shimon Bar Yochai."

The news stunned him. "Of course," he muttered to himself. "Let's drive to Mount Meron. I have a feeling something is going to happen there."

"What could possibly happen at a routine event?" she remarked dismissively.

"A mass casualty event. We must get there."

"How do you know?"

"Gut feeling," he replied.

"But I have plans; I need to work on the article."

"The corruption won't disappear; we'll return to it tomorrow."

"Fine. Though I think it's going to be a complete waste of time," she said, changing her route.

When they arrived at Mount Meron, they parked the car in the lower parking lot at the foot of the mountain and walked up. In a short time, they found themselves in a swarm of believers making their way up.

Upon reaching the top of the mountain, Hezi and Tamar found a large tree and sat under it, waiting for the evening and the central bonfire lighting ceremony, which marked the beginning of the Lag B'Omer celebrations. Thousands of ultra-Orthodox men, dressed in black suits and wearing black hats, gathered around the plaza, eagerly awaiting the ceremony.

"Do you want me to get you a cup of coffee?" he asked Tamar.

"Yes."

Hezi went and returned shortly with two cups of coffee, handed her one, and sat down beside her.

"Thank you," she said.

Hezi smiled in silence.

"Are you married?" she asked unexpectedly.

"No, I live with my girlfriend. And you?"

"I'm picky. I don't settle. That's why I'm still alone."

"I believe you'll find the right partner for you. It's just a matter of time."

Tamar smiled but said nothing.

Evening fell, and more people gathered around the plaza near the grave of Rabbi Shimon Bar Yochai. The ultra-Orthodox crowded together—families and individuals searching for answers and perhaps a blessing for a good life—trying to get inside, to touch the aura, to be part of the joy and revelry.

"Come on, we need to find a good spot to document the event."

Hezi stood up, reached out his hand, and helped Tamar to her feet. The two entered the complex, looking for a good spot to photograph and document the occasion.

"Last year, the event didn't take place because of the deadly pandemic. This year, it seems more people have come than expected," Tamar remarked.

"True. That's why I have a bad feeling that a disaster is about to happen," he replied.

Hezi found an old structure they could climb to get a view of the event from above. Unfortunately, he wasn't alone; other curious onlookers were also present. Hezi helped Tamar climb up, and they observed the scene together.

The hours passed slowly. It didn't seem like anything dramatic was about to happen. The feeling that the dream had been just a false alarm began to gnaw at him. Hezi feared Tamar would lose patience and want to return home in anger, thinking she shouldn't have listened to him in the first place.

As midnight approached, Tamar grew frustrated and tired, starting to lose her patience.

Hezi apologized, "I thought something would happen. I had a feeling. I disappointed you, didn't I?"

Tamar looked at him in stony silence. Hezi knew this was a bad sign; he would hear from her later. He secretly hoped she wouldn't fire him as she had his predecessors.

After midnight, when the ceremony ended, the crowd began to exit the complex through a long, narrow passage lined on both sides.

"They're starting to leave. Look over there," he pointed toward the distant exit.

Tamar wasn't impressed; she sank into despair, and anger boiled within her.

Hezi pulled out his camera and aimed it at the exit. More and more ultra-Orthodox crowded together, trying to pass through, but it was impossible. Within a short time, pushing began.

Hezi started taking photos while Tamar watched the scene with indifference.

The ultra-Orthodox began to feel suffocated. Some fell to the ground, and those behind them trampled over them, falling on top of them. Cries of distress echoed all around, but no help was in sight.

Hezi kept taking pictures, and suddenly, Tamar began to show interest in the event. She was no longer angry and started becoming active. She pulled out her notebook and documented in writing what she saw.

Half an hour passed. Those who had been trampled met their fate. When the rescue forces arrived, Hezi handed the camera to Tamar and said, "I'm going to help the rescue forces evacuate the injured."

Tamar nodded in agreement.

When he got there, he saw a horrific scene. Bodies lay on the ground, and the injured screamed in pain. Hezi helped evacuate the injured to the nearby ambulances.

A police car arrived shortly after, and two officers got out to maintain order. One of them, Oren, recognized Hezi.

"It's you again," he said, surprised. "First at the hit-and-run incident at the intersection, and now here."

"Now I'm in photographer mode," Hezi replied with a slight smile.

"I'm glad you're helping."

"Thank you."

After an hour, he returned to Tamar, who was very exhausted. "It's time to go," he said.

Tamar fell asleep, and Hezi drove all the way home. When they arrived, Tamar moved to the driver's seat, said goodbye, and continued to her home.

It was four in the morning. Hezi carefully opened the door and found Keren sitting and watching a movie.

"You're not asleep?" he remarked, surprised.

"I was waiting for you. Where were you? I was worried."

"I was at work; there was a mass casualty event at Mount Meron. You'll hear about it in the news. I need to sleep; it was an exhausting day."

Keren turned off the TV, switched off the lights, and went to bed with him.

Chapter 15

Hezi woke up in the late afternoon, exhausted and worn out from the previous day. He glanced at the bed and noticed the empty space beside him. He assumed Keren had hurried to get up early in the morning and had already left for work. Hezi got up, dressed, drank his coffee, and rushed out of the house to work.

When he arrived at the press building, he was surprised by the numerous compliments he received on the photos he had taken. Gidon, the editor, invited him to his office and proudly showed him the morning newspaper's headline. "That's your photo," he pointed out excitedly. Hezi smiled in response. "How did you know something would happen there?" "Just a hunch," he lied. "Well, your instincts were right."

Hezi went to Tamar's station and found her working on a new article. When she noticed him, she said, "Get ready; in half an hour, we're going to interview Minister of Public Security Tomer Cohen about his failures at Mount Meron." Hezi followed her instructions and went to fetch his photography equipment.

For the first time in his life, Hezi had the opportunity to meet a minister—in his office, no less. He packed the equipment into the trunk and sat, as usual, next to Tamar. When they entered the minister's office, Tamar sat down in front of the minister and prepared for the interview while Hezi set up his photography gear. As he did, he looked around, amazed at the number of people surrounding the minister—advisors, secretaries, politicians, and lobbyists who came and went as they pleased.

Tamar began the interview, and Hezi started taking pictures. The minister tried to keep his composure until Tamar attacked him, accusing him of horrific failures that led to many deaths. At one point, the minister appeared stressed and began to defend himself, making excuses as he shifted uncomfortably in his chair. "I accept responsibility for the incident, but I am not to blame," he said defensively, looking desperate. "Don't you think you should resign? Forty-five people lost their lives," she pressed again, not letting up. "No," he replied shortly.

Hezi took pictures of Minister Cohen from every possible angle, both up close and from a distance. After the interview, Tamar bid the minister goodbye, left his office, and muttered into the air, "Just shameful." Hezi trailed behind her.

On the way back to the car, she said, "I need a drink. There's a bar nearby. Do you want to join me?" "Sure," he replied, and got into the car.

The car stopped near a secluded neighborhood bar. Tamar got out and walked toward the bar, and Hezi joined her. The bar was empty. The two of them sat on round wooden stools near the counter and ordered beers. The bartender quickly arrived with two full glasses and placed them beside them. Tamar took a sip of her beer, sighed, and muttered, "What a tiring day." Hezi also took a sip without saying a word.

"Whenever I interview politicians, I always assume they're going to lie and try to deceive me. You can't believe a word that comes out of their mouths. One day they're for something, the next day they're against it, and on the third day they abstain. One day they'll make a promise, and you'll believe them, and the next day they'll break that promise and claim they don't remember making it." "Don't take it personally; that's the game—political survival," he replied. "Political survival at the expense of the public." "Yes, unfortunately."

Tamar turned to him and asked, "If you promised something, would you break your promise?" "Only if I was backed into a corner. Fortunately, I'm not a politician. I usually try to keep my promises; otherwise, they have no meaning." "Exactly. You're an honest and straightforward person. I like that." They finished their beers.

"I'm finishing early today. Would you like to come over?" she asked. "No, I'd rather go home and rest." "Of course," she replied with a forced smile.

Hezi returned home, and it was nine in the evening. The house was empty. He found a note on the fridge that read, "Went to visit my parents; I'll be back later." He wasn't surprised; Keren occasionally visited her parents during the week. Hezi opened the fridge and saw that there was almost nothing to eat. He took out a spread, made himself a sandwich, and sat down to watch TV alone. The hours passed, it got late, but Keren still hadn't arrived. He began to worry and decided to call her, only to find that she had left her phone at home. He wasn't surprised this time either. He took a shower and went to bed. When Keren returned at midnight, Hezi was already fast asleep.

***

The weekend arrived sooner than expected. Hezi left his house early in the morning for a long walk along the promenade, dressed in workout clothes. The weather was pleasant, and the heat was bearable. At this hour, the avenue was almost empty. Midway through his walk, he suddenly saw a shadow of wings growing behind him until he felt a thump on his head. Hezi noticed a crow that had flown over him and landed in front of him on the ground.

Hezi felt his head to make sure he wasn't injured. When he realized everything was fine, he wondered if he should react to the crow's audacity and throw something at it. But on second thought, he decided not to get into trouble with it. After all, it's known that crows avenge anyone who harms them, and they're very hard to get rid of. Hezi passed the crow and continued his walk until he returned home.

Keren had just woken up, and Hezi told her about the strange incident. "It's good you didn't react," she declared. "Do you want to go to the beach later?" he asked. "No, I can't come. Maybe another time." Hezi looked disappointed; he had hoped for a warmer response. "Is something wrong?" he asked. "No, I'm just not clean, if you understand." Hezi nodded. "We can do something else if you'd like," he suggested. "Maybe later; I planned to read a book," she replied.

Hezi arrived for another routine workday, as much as his job could be called routine, given that every day was different and held unpleasant surprises. He made himself coffee and went to Tamar's station. He noticed her typing up a memo for an article she was preparing. Tamar waved at him and signaled for him to sit beside her. When she finished, she said, "We have an interesting day at court. Today, there's supposed to be a ruling on whether Jews can return to their homes and live in the Sheikh Jarrah neighborhood in the heart of the Arab population in East Jerusalem—a very volatile case."

"That's not good. It means there will be riots," he predicted.

"Yes," she smiled. "And that's your chance to capture a winning shot."

Hezi didn't seem enthusiastic. "Isn't it dangerous?"

"Yes. We'll need to take protective measures—helmet and bulletproof vest. You're not scared, are you?"

"Me? Not at all," he lied, hoping Tamar wouldn't notice his expression. Then he went to the storage room, grabbed the photography and protective gear, and joined Tamar for the ride.

When they arrived at the courthouse, they saw an Arab crowd protesting at the entrance, shouting hateful slogans: "With blood and fire, we will redeem..." Tamar parked the car, and they both got out and put on their protective gear. Hezi positioned himself with his camera at a good vantage point.

An hour later, Attorney Mansour, representing the Arab sector against the state, came out of the courthouse and announced to the protesters and the media that he had failed to change the judges' ruling. The inflamed crowd raised signs and loudly chanted, "Allahu Akbar" (God is great). Tamar interviewed one of the angry protesters, who said that the Arab public would not remain silent, and a response would come. Hezi photographed him and the protesters from every possible angle.

One of the protesters pushed Tamar. She stumbled and fell to the ground. Hezi put the camera on the floor and quickly helped her up. "Are you okay? Did you get hurt?" he asked. Tamar smiled. "I'm fine. I'm used to it." Hezi wrapped his arm around her waist and helped her up, walking her to the car parked by the roadside. "I see you got injured on your leg," he said. "We should find a nearby pharmacy; you need to bandage the wound." Hezi seated Tamar in the car, got behind the wheel, and started driving. A few blocks away, he found a pharmacy. He parked the car, went inside, bought a bandage and disinfectant, and returned to the car to bandage her leg. "Thanks," she said with a smile, placing her hand on his. Hezi gently pulled his hand away. "We should get going," he said. Tamar nodded in agreement.

During the drive, she suddenly asked, "Do you enjoy working with me?"

"Yes. There's never a dull moment. The job is challenging," he replied with a smile.

"Good, because the challenges have only just begun." Hezi didn't really dwell on the meaning of her words; he wanted to get to the office as quickly as possible to drop Tamar off and then head home. Tamar leaned on Hezi as she made her way to her station. She carefully sat down in her chair and then said goodbye to him.

Hezi returned home and found Keren baking cookies in the kitchen. "Do you want to go to a movie or eat at a restaurant?" he asked.

"Not today. Maybe over the weekend. I have to wake up early tomorrow," she replied.

Hezi looked disappointed. He had hoped to go out and unwind from the busy day he had. He wanted to be with Keren, whose company he missed so much.

"I feel like you're constantly avoiding and distancing yourself from me. You're not paying attention to me," he began.

"I had a tough week at work; you need to understand that."

Hezi couldn't understand; he couldn't grasp how Keren hadn't found the time to spend with him, not even a single hour.

Looking particularly hurt, he left angrily and went to take a shower to refresh himself.

In the evening, he watched the news, despite having already experienced enough events for the day.

Riots had begun in Jerusalem. Arabs from the eastern part of the city harassed passersby in the Old City and proudly uploaded videos to social media.

He heard the leader of Hamas threatening Israel, saying that he would not allow Jews to enter the Sheikh Jarrah neighborhood, and if that happened, he would bombard the country with rockets.

Hezi knew the atmosphere was volatile, and it was only a matter of time before violence erupted in the streets. It wouldn't be long before he had to drag himself with his camera into the angry crowd and try to document the riots and violence from every possible angle, risking his life.

Despite his love for photography, he was far from enthusiastic about it.

It was late. Hezi turned off the TV and went to bed.

Keren had already fallen asleep, turning her back to him.

Hezi once again had a vivid and frightening dream, just like the previous ones. In the dream, he saw a stage collapsing and people dressed in black falling to their deaths.

Hezi woke up in a panic, went to the refrigerator, took out some water, sat on the couch, and drank thirstily. He tried to think about where he had seen the terrifying scene, but the clues seemed vague. He assumed it might have happened inside a synagogue.

Chapter 16

In the morning, when he woke up, Keren was already at work. Hezi quickly got ready and left the house. When he arrived at the office, he saw Tamar chatting and joking with colleagues—something she didn't usually do since she was always busy.

Curious, Hezi approached her and asked, "Did something happen?"

"I'm celebrating my birthday this evening at my place. I invited some colleagues from work to celebrate with me. You're, of course, invited too," she said with a smile.

"Happy birthday. I'll come," he said and then asked curiously, "How old are you?"

"You shouldn't ask a woman that question, but I'll let you guess."

Hezi refrained from guessing, although he estimated that she was about his age. Tamar left the group and headed to her desk, with Hezi following. When they sat down, he said, "Do you remember the disaster at Mount Meron?"

"Yes, the disaster where all the responsible parties refused to take accountability."

Hezi nodded, looking around to ensure no one was listening.

"I have a feeling that another similar disaster is about to happen."

"Your instincts are starting to scare me. Where?"

"I don't know. Probably in some ultra-Orthodox neighborhood."

Tamar stood up. "Let's switch. Sit at my desk near the computer and try to remember."

Hezi did as she suggested and tried searching for clues on the computer, but after half an hour, he came up empty-handed.

"I can't find anything."

"Let's take a walk around the city streets, you and me. What do you say?"

"Alright."

"Bring your camera equipment, just in case," she instructed him.

Tamar drove as usual. First, they headed toward Mea Shearim neighborhood. As they got closer, Hezi shook his head.

"Maybe Ramat Shlomo," she suggested.

"I don't know; the clues are vague—nothing more," he replied.

"Close your eyes; try to remember. We have time."

Tamar parked her car near the sidewalk of a quiet street.

"I'm going to get us some coffee in the meantime," she said, leaving the car.

Hezi closed his eyes and tried to recall details from the dream, but to no avail.

Tamar returned with two cups of coffee and pastries, handing him one of the cups.

"So, did you manage to remember?" she asked.

"No."

"You still seem troubled," she observed.

"Yes, but it's something personal."

"Tell me; I know how to keep a secret."

Hezi hesitated, took a sip of his coffee, and remained silent, contemplating whether to share. Finally, he decided.

"My girlfriend has been distant lately. I try to talk to her, but she keeps avoiding me. I don't know what to do."

"She's probably going through something. You need to be patient with her—give her time. Sooner or later, she'll tell you," she said, thinking to herself that this was her chance to win his heart again.

Hezi sat in thought and then suggested they return to the office since he believed there was little chance he would know where the event would occur.

Tamar had a different idea.

"Let's go to the Mahane Yehuda market. I've always wanted to visit there. Besides, we have some time before we get called to another assignment—let's make the most of it," she said.

Hezi didn't like crowded places; they made him anxious. The presence of security personnel in the area didn't calm him but had the opposite effect.

He remembered that, in the distant past, terrorists used to plant bombs under the stalls. The terror attack he had experienced left scars on his soul that were unlikely to heal anytime soon.

Shavuot was approaching. Many people were coming to buy food for the holiday, and the crowd was noticeable. He heard the vendors' voices, smelled the spices, and silently prayed to get out of there safely.

Tamar made her way through the market, examining the various stalls, and even bought spices, halva, and a bottle of olive oil.

Hezi followed her, looking around with heavy apprehension.

At some point, Hezi felt that every step he took became slower, as if he were walking through a swamp.

He stopped in his tracks and couldn't move, his legs rooted deeply to the ground like a tree. He began to panic and sweat.

Tamar didn't notice, but when she saw him far behind her, about to be swallowed by the crowd surrounding him from all sides, she quickly returned to him.

"What's wrong?" she asked with concern.

Hezi struggled to breathe; fear paralyzed him. He managed to say only, "I can't breathe."

"Let's get out of here," she said, taking his hand in hers and pulling him out of the market. Once they had walked a few steps away, she said, "Breathe deeply and exhale the air out. Repeat the process several times until you calm down."

Hezi followed her instructions, and gradually he returned to himself. They sat down on the sidewalk, with Tamar still holding his hand.

"I didn't know you were so scared."

"Neither did I. It probably started after the traumatic event I went through."

"What event?"

Hezi told her about the terror attack at the restaurant that occurred while he was dining with his girlfriend, Keren—the prolonged hospitalization and the lengthy recovery period he went through at the hospital.

Tamar remembered the event because she had covered it extensively. She hurried to get him a bottle of mineral water.

"Drink; it'll make you feel better," she said.

Hezi drank from the bottle thirstily, and his spirits returned.

"We should head back to the press building," she remarked. Hezi nodded in agreement.

In the evening, Hezi informed Keren that he had been invited to a birthday party for a colleague named Tamar, along with other invitees. Keren asked when he would be back.

"Around midnight, I guess."

"Have fun."

"Thanks," he replied briefly.

Hezi dressed nicely, said goodbye to Keren, and left the house. On the way, he bought a bottle of wine so as not to arrive empty-handed. Tamar's apartment was in an old four-story building without an elevator on the outskirts of the city.

Hezi climbed to the third floor, stood in front of the door, and rang the bell. Tamar opened the door. She was wearing a revealing evening dress and looked particularly groomed. She smiled at him, took the bottle of wine from his hands, and invited him inside.

Hezi entered, examining his surroundings. The living room looked small and modest, with a sofa, a table, an old sideboard with a large TV on it, and a single modern picture hanging on a white wall. Near the wall was a table with a cake, drinks, and snacks.

"Where is everyone?" he asked.

"They'll be here soon. Come with me; I'll give you a tour of the house." Tamar showed him the two small rooms: a simple bedroom with a double bed where she slept and another bedroom with a single bed, connected by a hallway.

Hezi had expected to find a well-furnished and stylish home, but it wasn't the case.

"Nice place," he finally said, just to be polite.

Suddenly, the doorbell rang. Tamar moved closer to him in the hallway, standing so near that he could feel her breath on his face, and his heart began to pound.

"Well, the guests have arrived," she smiled and went to open the door.

Hezi breathed a sigh of relief and followed her to the living room.

More and more guests arrived at her home. Many of them Hezi recognized from the office. Most arrived empty-handed but made sure to wish her a happy birthday and seemed genuinely happy for her.

Tamar mingled with the guests, laughing with them and exchanging stories. Hezi watched her curiously from the sidelines, getting to know another side of her—one that was more sociable.

Occasionally, they exchanged brief glances.

After about half an hour, Tamar approached the cake, cut it into slices, and handed them out to the guests.

"I saved the best piece for you," she said to Hezi with a wink, adding, "With the cherry on top."

Tamar continued socializing with the guests while Hezi remained alone on the sofa, feeling somewhat awkward. Although one of the guests occasionally struck up a friendly conversation with him, most of the time, he felt lonely and not quite part of the group.

At midnight, when most of the guests were still celebrating, Hezi approached Tamar and told her he was going home. Tamar seemed to be in high spirits after drinking alcohol.

"Already?" she asked, moving so close that he could smell the alcohol on her breath.

"It's late, and I'm also tired."

"Alright. I'll forgive you this time," she said, waving goodbye and returning to the guests.

Hezi left her home and quickly headed back to his, not wanting Keren to worry or think that something had happened to him on the way.

When he entered, he saw Keren watching TV. He wasn't surprised that she stayed up late.

"How was it?" she asked.

"It was nice. I'm tired; I'm going to sleep."

Keren turned off the TV and also went to bed.

Chapter 17

Shavuot arrived, and Hezi prepared for the holiday, hoping to celebrate with his partner at a festive meal he had worked on beforehand. Suddenly, he heard his mobile phone ringing and quickly answered. On the line was Tamar.

"Come to work quickly; there's been a disaster."

"What happened?" he asked, curiosity piquing his interest.

"Just come; we'll talk later," she replied.

Hezi looked disappointed; his plans for a festive evening were dashed. He approached Keren, who was arranging clothes in the closet.

"I have to go to work. It's an emergency."

"I thought we were going to celebrate the holiday together," she said, disappointment evident in her voice.

"Me too. There's never a dull moment in this country," he said as he left the house.

The newsroom appeared hectic. Reporters were talking among themselves and exchanging impressions about an event that had occurred. The editor-in-chief's office looked chaotic and crowded with people.

"What happened?" Hezi asked Tamar, still curious.

"You arrived just in time. Grab your equipment, and we'll go. I'll tell you on the way."

Hezi quickly brought his camera equipment and got into the car. Tamar started the engine and began driving.

"You were right, and I didn't believe it," she muttered.

"I don't understand," he said.

"You said there would be casualties at a synagogue in one of the Haredi neighborhoods in Jerusalem. Well, it happened; there's been a report of many casualties in Givat Ze'ev. We need to hurry."

"Drive carefully; that's more important," he remarked.

"How did you know this would happen?

"Simple logic. Holidays during the coronavirus pandemic are always prone to disaster. Many people don't follow health guidelines and ignore proper safety measures. Just like what happened at Mount Meron—crowding in confined spaces leads to tragedies, and who doesn't want to celebrate?"

"Everyone wants to," she replied.

"Even in synagogues, they celebrate, with crowding and jostling," he added, hoping Tamar would be satisfied with his explanation and not press further. But Tamar wasn't convinced. She remembered that he hadn't mentioned the holiday the last time they talked about the event, only a vague feeling. She decided to stay silent for now.

As they entered Givat Ze'ev, traffic congestion started to build. The delay stretched on, and it seemed like Tamar was still far from her destination. Eventually, she gave up and parked the car on a nearby street.

"It looks like we'll need to walk from here; there's no other choice," she said.

Tamar managed to slip through the police blockade but was pushed back when a stern-faced officer noticed her. Frustrated, she searched for random witnesses to describe what had happened. She found a kind paramedic who explained the event to her.

"Yeshiva students were standing on a stage in the synagogue, and the stage collapsed with everyone on it. There are many injuries and perhaps even fatalities."

A Haredi woman passing by told Tamar that the synagogue had been recently renovated.

Tamar summarized the event for Hezi. "Once again, we are witnesses to a disaster caused by criminal negligence. I wonder how the minister will react when he hears about another disaster. And maybe this is just the beginning; who knows? There's no accountability, no lessons learned, and the world goes on as usual."

"We know, don't we?" he replied.

He sat on the sidewalk far from the curious

"Take some pictures of the victims and the scene, and then we'll leave. There's no downtime."

Hezi tried to find a promising angle for a shot. He squeezed through the crowd of onlookers and almost reached the scene when a short-tempered Haredi man in his twenties became angry at him, hit him in rage, and knocked his camera to the ground.

Hezi stepped back, his camera broken and blood dripping from his nose. He gathered the camera pieces, navigated his way back through the crowd, and exited.

"What happened to you?" Tamar asked when she saw him.

"A hot-tempered Haredi man attacked me," he explained.

"You need to get treated."

"It's nothing," he replied, holding his bleeding nose.

"We'll go to my place, and I'll take care of you. We need to stop the bleeding."

Hezi tried to explain that it wasn't necessary, but Tamar insisted. When they arrived at her place, Tamar asked Hezi to lie on the couch. She quickly fetched a bandage, sat beside him, and bandaged his nose.

"Would you like some water?" she asked.

"Yes, thank you."

After she brought him water, she noticed her shirt was stained with blood.

"I'm going to change my shirt," she said and went to her room.

Hezi drank the water gratefully, set the glass down, and closed his eyes to relax a bit. After a few moments, he felt a gentle hand caressing his chest. He opened his eyes and saw Tamar sitting next to him, gently caressing him. He noticed her chest peeking out from under her shirt. His body wanted to indulge in the excitement, but at the same time, his conscience chastised him.

"I can't," he said, removing her hand. "You're an attractive woman, but right now, I'm not available."

Tamar smiled at him. "Of course, I'm patient."

Hezi gathered himself and soon sat up on the couch. "I need to go," he said, getting up from the couch, saying goodbye to her, and heading home. On the way, doubts arose in his mind. Hezi began questioning whether he had acted correctly in rejecting her and, while convincing himself, gave himself answers.

***

Hezi watched TV with concern. The Hamas organization, which controls Gaza, explicitly threatened to launch rockets at Israel in protest of what they called "the Israeli attempt to take over East Jerusalem." The announcement left no doubt that it was only a matter of time before Israeli cities would be bombarded.

Hezi secretly hoped that this event would not happen in the coming days. He feared the scenes he would witness would be difficult for him—scenes of damage to property and people that he would have to document in those bombarded cities.

The very next morning, alarms sounded across Jerusalem, and several rockets fired toward the city were intercepted by the Iron Dome defense system. The conflict did not end there. Israel responded with rocket fire toward Gaza, demolishing high-rise buildings that were unoccupied at the time. An unending cycle of fighting began.

Alarms were sounded in other cities, and unfortunately, there were direct hits on homes, causing property damage and sometimes even casualties.

Hezi was summoned from his home multiple times and sometimes had to spend a lot of time at the newsroom. Every time an alarm sounded; he took cover with other reporters in the stairwell. Occasionally, he and Tamar would go to the field to visit damaged sites. He documented the events with his camera while Tamar interviewed those suffering from anxiety.

Sometimes, the alarms would catch them during an interview with one of the victims, forcing them to stop in the middle and run to seek shelter in a nearby bomb shelter, waiting for the storm to pass. The sounds of explosions were sometimes heard directly above their heads, prompting them to lie on the floor with their hands over their heads, praying that the shells wouldn't hit them.

Each time, Hezi felt paralyzed and struggled to breathe. Tamar had to hold him and speak soothingly until he calmed down, recovered, and continued to document the difficult scenes.

"Thank you," he said to her. "What would I do without you?"

"I'm sure you would have acted just like me," she replied with a smile.

On one occasion, they arrived at a family's home that had been completely destroyed, but the family had miraculously survived.

"Don't forget to photograph them against the backdrop of the ruins," Tamar instructed Hezi.

"Can you tell us how you survived?" Tamar asked the anxious and frightened mother of the house.

"We heard the alarm and ran to the protected space. When we came out, there was nothing left; everything was destroyed."

Tamar recorded her words. She asked the woman for permission to photograph the ruins from inside the house, but the rescue forces who arrived pushed her back along with all the onlookers, asking everyone to return to their homes and stay in the protected space.

Hezi felt suffocated frequently; too many events had happened in the past year. First, the terrorist attack where he was critically injured and hospitalized for an extended period, then the mysterious pandemic that forced him to stay home for a long time, and now the relentless fighting, which was too much for him.

He sat on the sidewalk, far from the curious onlookers, placing his camera beside him as he struggled to catch his breath. Tamar arrived quickly, sitting down beside him and trying to calm him.

"You should drink some water," she said, handing him the bottle.

"Thank you," he replied, drinking gratefully.

"Let's go to a quieter place," she suggested.

"But where? There are alarms everywhere."

"Not everywhere. There are still places where you can breathe without fear," she replied with a smile.

"Where?"

"I'll take you to your home."

"No, no, that's not a good idea," he answered anxiously, fearing that Keren might notice her, and he would have a hard time explaining.

"You have nothing to fear. I promise I'll be on my best behavior," she said.

Hezi considered her words. He preferred to return home alone, but in his condition, he couldn't drive.

"Okay, but only to my house."

"Alright."

When they arrived at his place, Tamar parked the car near the building.

"So, this is where you live," she remarked.

"Yes, on the third floor."

Tamar looked up; the balcony was open, and she inferred that Keren was home.

Hezi said goodbye to her and went back to his apartment.

Chapter 18

The sirens didn't stop, even at odd hours. Hezi woke up in a panic at four in the morning, roused Keren, and together they rushed to the safe room. Sometimes the sirens blared at six in the morning, sometimes later. Hezi was suffering from a lack of sleep, feeling exhausted and struggling to function. At times, he drank several cups of coffee to stay alert.

During those days, riots broke out in mixed cities where Jews and Arabs lived together. Until that time, the residents had lived in admirable coexistence. But now, that coexistence shattered, suspicion spread everywhere, and hatred reared its head. Young

Muslim rioters took to the streets, setting shops and cars on fire and attacking innocent passersby, some of whom lost their lives. Many barricaded themselves in their homes out of fear.

Hezi soon realized that a difficult and challenging period lay ahead, and he would have to spend long hours outside, risking his life in pursuit of the perfect shot that would capture the violent events and make the front pages. As he pondered this, Tamar called and asked him to come quickly to the press building. Hezi did as she instructed.

It was late afternoon, and the journalists were busy preparing the stories that would appear the next morning. Hezi noticed them contacting field reporters to get updates on the ongoing situation. Gideon was surrounded in his office by men and women eager to pitch their stories for the front page. He appeared overwhelmed, struggling to focus amid the noise, and asked them to step outside and wait their turn patiently.

Hezi reached Tamar's desk and found her talking on her mobile phone. She gestured for him to sit. He sat and waited patiently until she finished her call. Tamar abruptly ended the conversation and said to him, "Go get the equipment, and bring protective gear too. We're moving out." She then resumed her conversation. Hezi did as she instructed and returned with the equipment to her desk.

"Let's go," she said while still on the phone. Unlike previous times, a sophisticated communication van with an additional crew was waiting for them. The two got in, and the van set off.

Hezi began to feel fear slowly creeping through his body. He was afraid of getting hurt by the rioters and didn't want to risk his life. He had been given a second chance at life and didn't intend to waste it on any story, no matter how important it was. Unfortunately, the job sometimes required it.

The drive took a long time due to heavy traffic. Hezi closed his eyes and silently prayed that everything would pass peacefully.

"Are you okay?" Tamar asked with concern after noticing him struggling to breathe.

Hezi smiled faintly.

"Keep breathing; it helps," she said.

The van stopped a few streets away from the scene of the incident. Hezi appeared slightly calmer.

"Come on, we need to move," she said.

The two got out of the van and heard distant shouting and nationalist slogans. As they got closer, the voices grew louder.

Tamar seemed confident and walked toward the noise. Hezi, on the other hand, felt very scared and lagged behind.

"Maybe we should keep our distance," he muttered.

"Don't worry; we'll stand in a safe spot," she replied.

The two walked toward the angry crowd. The other pair who had been in the van with them split off in a different direction.

Tamar entered a nearby building and climbed the stairs to the first floor. Hezi followed her without asking any unnecessary questions, carrying all the photography equipment on his back.

Tamar knocked on one of the doors. A woman in her forties opened it cautiously. Tamar showed her press credentials.

"Can we cover the event from your apartment? It won't take long," she asked.

"Okay," the woman replied reluctantly.

The two entered and went straight to the balcony. Alongside the homeowner, they watched as the angry crowd vented its rage on nearby cars and shops—smashing windows, setting things on fire, and attacking passersby.

Hezi searched for a good angle and captured the scene with his camera.

An hour later, the police arrived in force, attempting to restore order and arrest the rioters.

"Let's go downstairs and try to get as close as possible. Maybe we can interview one of the rioters," Tamar suggested.

Hezi began to feel anxious but tried to mask it.

They cautiously approached the edge of the crowd. Tamar singled out one of the rioters and introduced herself as a journalist. He refused to cooperate, shouting only, "Al-Aqsa is in danger! Millions of martyrs are marching to Al-Quds (Jerusalem)!"

Another protester, caught in the frenzy, tried to hit her in anger. Hezi stepped in to shield her, taking a punch to the face. He fell to the ground, terrified the crowd might turn on him.

Tamar quickly helped him up. "I'm sorry, that was a mistake. We took too big a risk. Let's find a safer spot."

They retreated from the crowd and took shelter inside one of the empty shops nearby.

Hours passed, yet the riot showed no signs of calming. It was already four in the morning. Both Hezi and Tamar were exhausted.

"There's a hostel nearby. Let's go sleep and come back later. It's an approved expense," Tamar suggested.

Hezi disliked the idea but, realizing there was no other choice, agreed reluctantly. "Okay," he replied.

They reached the Crossroads Hostel, tucked away in a quieter area a few streets from the unrest. At the reception desk, they booked a room.

Hezi lay down on the bed and immediately slipped into a deep sleep. He was so exhausted that he didn't notice the sunlight filtering through the blinds, illuminating the dreary room, nor the birds chirping to announce the early afternoon.

Gradually, a sense of unease stirred within him. He opened his eyes groggily, checked his watch—and was shocked to find it was already two in the afternoon.

Next to him, Tamar was still asleep, her hand resting on his chest. As he became more aware, he noticed she was only in her underwear. Panic surged through him.

He glanced down at himself and was stunned to see he, too, was stripped to just his underwear. Heart racing, he gently moved her hand aside, sat up, and frantically scanned the room for their clothes but couldn't find them.

"Tamar, wake up," he whispered, nudging her shoulder. After a few attempts, she opened her eyes groggily.

"What happened? Why am I undressed?" he demanded, his voice edged with alarm.

"You're telling me you don't remember anything?" she asked with a playful smirk.

"No," he answered flatly.

"Well, it was an unforgettable night."

"Did we... have sex?" he asked nervously.

"No, silly," she laughed. "You fell asleep right away, and I had to take off both our clothes. They were filthy and reeked of smoke." She gave him a teasing look. "Now you can put them back on. But there's still time, if you want..." she added with a playful hint, placing her hand on his abdomen.

"No, there's no time," he replied, moving her hand aside as he wrapped himself in a blanket and searched for his clothes.

"Too bad," she murmured with a mischievous smile, getting up to dress.

Hezi dressed quickly, trying to focus, while Tamar moved slowly, unconcerned. He avoided looking at her, but curiosity got the better of him. He stole a glance, only to meet her gaze—playful, inviting, and full of intent.

After they were dressed, Hezi asked, "Are we going home?"

"No. We're going to have lunch and then back to work," she replied.

Hezi stepped out of the room and quickly called Keren. He tried to reassure her, explaining that the violent events he was documenting required him to work irregular hours. He promised to make it up to her when everything settled down.

The two left the hostel, walked down the main street, and entered a nearby restaurant. In the distance, the sounds of protesters shouting echoed, while the sky remained heavy with smoke.

Hezi sat across from Tamar and began eating. As he ate, unbidden thoughts of her naked body returned, stirring desires he tried to suppress. He wondered how much longer he could resist such temptations—how long before his self-control gave out.

Maybe he should quit his job. Though he enjoyed the work, even with all its risks, leaving might be the only way to avoid a mistake he couldn't take back. But what then? If he quit, he'd be back home, stuck in frustration, waiting for another, less demanding job to come along.

He tried not to look directly at Tamar, hoping to avoid any conversations about the thoughts swirling in his mind.

"Prepare yourself. If the unrest continues, we might have to stay another day," Tamar said, breaking his train of thought.

"Another day," he repeated, his voice heavy with disappointment.

"Think we'll ever have a day when nothing happens, and the news will report something light? Maybe dolphins swimming off the Israeli coast?"

"They might mention dolphins—briefly," Hezi replied. "But the focus will always be on scandals and secret military operations."

"You're such an optimist," Tamar teased.

"I try," he muttered.

"Are you done? It's time to get back to the battlefield," she said, rising from her seat.

On the nearby street, the crowd swelled as more protesters arrived. Tamar and Hezi stood on the sidelines, documenting the chaos. The second day of riots was in full swing. Reinforcements arrived—mounted officers among them—intent on quelling the unrest.

Hezi hoped things wouldn't spiral into a bloodbath, but it quickly became clear his fears were well-founded. The riot intensified, with scenes of looted shops, burning cars, and attacks on innocent bystanders.

Hezi captured moments of terror and desperation through his camera lens, while Tamar interviewed police officers struggling to restore order.

At one point, Hezi recognized a familiar face—a police officer he'd met before under tragic circumstances.

"You again," the officer said with a grin. "I'm starting to think you've got some insider info."

"You know, it's not exactly fun when you keep saying that," Hezi grumbled.

"Just messing with you," the officer chuckled, then returned to his duties.

Night fell slowly, and the streets were blanketed in flickering streetlights, casting pale glows over the bloodied ground. Young men clashed with police, who fought back with tear gas. Ambulances raced through the streets, sirens blaring, carrying the injured to hospitals.

Hezi grew weary. Hours of standing and documenting the violence wore him down. He prayed he wouldn't get caught by a hotheaded rioter and suffer another beating or worse.

By two in the morning, he could barely keep his eyes open.

"I'm exhausted," he told Tamar. "I'm about to pass out."

"Alright. We've got what we need for the report. Let's head back to the hostel," she agreed.

When they reached the room, Hezi hoped to collapse into bed and sleep through the night. But Tamar had other plans.

"You can't get into a clean bed smelling like that. Take a shower first," she instructed.

Hezi groaned but knew she was right. Reluctantly, he entered the bathroom, stripped off his clothes, and stood under the hot water. He closed his eyes, letting the warmth wash away the grime and sweat.

A few minutes later, the bathroom door creaked open. Hezi didn't notice until he felt a hand slide over his back. Startled, he opened his eyes—and there she was, naked, smiling mischievously.

"You forgot the soap," Tamar said, holding up the bottle.

"Here, let me help. You'll see—it'll feel good."

"Thanks, but I can handle it," Hezi replied, trying to sound firm.

"Don't be silly," she whispered, stepping into the shower with him.

She poured the blue liquid into her hands and began rubbing it over his body. Hezi clenched his jaw, struggling against the desire that surged within him.

Guilt gnawed at him, warning him to stop, but her touch was relentless. His resolve faltered. He closed his eyes as her hand slid lower, pausing over his genitals. His heart pounded. He felt himself harden.

Tamar pressed her body against his, the water cascading over them. She kissed his lips and neck with deliberate intensity, like a predator closing in on its prey.

Hezi's breath hitched. Panic fought with desire, but Tamar didn't let him pull away. He felt himself enter her, their bodies moving in sync. And in that moment, he gave in completely.

When it was over, the water still flowed, but the moment felt heavy with finality. The deed was done.

Now came the regret—the guilt that would haunt him, inescapable and unforgiving.

Chapter 19

Hezi slept so deeply that he thought the wild night he had experienced was just an erotic dream. But as the fog of sleep lifted, he cautiously opened his eyes, hoping for the best. To his dismay, it wasn't a dream. He found himself lying naked in bed with Tamar, who was also naked, her arm draped around him in an embrace.

He quickly moved her hand aside, got up, and dressed hurriedly.

"Tamar, wake up," he said, nudging her shoulder. "I'm heading home."

Tamar stirred but resisted fully waking.

"Want me to drive you?" she asked groggily.

"No, I have to go."

"Alright, I'll call you later."

Hezi slipped out of the room and hurried home, his thoughts swirling. Should he tell Keren about what happened? No. She wouldn't understand. It was just a one-time thing—better to keep it to himself. No one needed to know. It would be easier that way, he convinced himself.

He entered his apartment quietly, even though he knew Keren was still at work. Closing the door softly behind him, he went straight to the bathroom, determined to wash away the guilt clinging to him. Under the hot stream, he told himself again and again: It was a mistake. It won't happen again. No one needs to know.

After showering, Hezi decided to cook a special lunch for Keren. It had been ages since he last prepared a meal for her, and he hoped it might make up for his long absences and late nights. As the aroma of food filled the air, he washed the dishes and waited in the living room for her to arrive.

Keren came home about thirty minutes later, bags in hand.

"I stopped to do some shopping," she said as she walked in.

When she reached the dining area, she saw the table beautifully set with an assortment of dishes.

"What a pleasant surprise," she remarked with a warm smile.

"I wanted to make it up to you for being away so much," Hezi replied, masking the truth behind his words.

Keren quickly put the groceries in the fridge, then joined him at the table, sitting across from him. Hezi hoped the rest of the day would be peaceful—no interruptions from Tamar, no more late-night assignments or seedy hostels. He was done with all of it. He had already decided: he was going to quit the job.

He watched Keren start eating.

"How is it?" he asked.

"Tasty," she replied, smiling.

"Glad you like it."

He hesitated, then spoke. "I'm thinking of quitting my job."

Keren looked at him curiously. "Tired of the tough scenes and crazy hours?"

"Yeah. It's getting to me."

"And what will you do? Stay home all day?"

"I'll find something else."

"I'll support whatever decision you make," she said, reaching out to touch his hand.

"Thanks," Hezi murmured, feeling both comforted and burdened by her trust.

For the rest of the day, Tamar didn't call. Relief washed over Hezi as he climbed into bed that night. But as soon as his head hit the pillow, guilt crept back in, gnawing at him, giving him no peace.

Keren curled up beside him, wanting to be close. Hezi responded willingly—it had been a long time since they'd been intimate, and he feared such moments might become rare. He tried to savor the warmth of her body, to let himself enjoy it. But despite his best efforts, flashes of Tamar's naked body flickered in his mind.

He fought against the memories, only to find they were stronger than he had imagined. Every time he pushed them down, they rose again, threatening to overwhelm him.

After a restless night of conflicting desires, Hezi finally fell into a deep sleep. But peace didn't last. In his dream, he saw an old woman—bruised, beaten—lying on a sidewalk, crying for help. She was alone, and no one came to her aid.

Hezi woke abruptly, heart pounding. Unlike before, he didn't push the dream aside. Instead, he grabbed a notebook from the bedside table and jotted down every detail he could recall—streets, houses, benches, shops, the time of day, anything that stood out.

One detail became clear in his mind: the location was a side street near a three-story building clad in gray marble tiles.

Satisfied that he had captured everything, Hezi put the notebook down, exhaled deeply, and drifted back to sleep, hoping that, for the remainder of the night, his dreams would leave him in peace.

Keren got up early as usual and headed to work. Hezi woke up later, got ready, and left the house to search for a place resembling the description he had written down the night before. He wandered for hours—crossing streets, ducking into alleys, strolling through parks—but found nothing that matched.

He began to wonder if the location was in another city, or if perhaps it had all been a product of his imagination. Frustrated, he scanned the surroundings one last time and, with a sigh, decided to head home.

Just as he started walking back, his phone rang. He glanced at the screen and sighed again. It was Tamar.

"Yes," he answered, his reluctance obvious.

"There's an operation planned for tonight," she said.

"What kind of operation?"

"Jewish extremists are organizing demonstrations against Arabs."

"No way," Hezi muttered, genuinely surprised.

"We've got reliable intel. Get some rest, and in the evening, come to the press building. We'll head out together to cover the event. It's going to be fascinating."

"Okay," he replied, though his enthusiasm was lacking.

As soon as the call ended, something caught his eye—an old woman, slowly making her way down the street, a shopping basket in hand. She looked eerily similar to the woman from his dream. Unsure if it was really her, Hezi decided to follow.

The woman turned into a dimly lit alley, one Hezi hadn't explored before. As he followed from a distance, his heart skipped a beat. He saw the house—the very one from his dream—exactly as he had pictured it, down to the smallest detail.

It had to be the same woman.

Then, out of the corner of his eye, Hezi noticed a young man loitering near the entrance of a nearby building, his posture tense, as if waiting for the perfect moment to strike.

Hezi's heart raced. Without hesitation, he hurried toward the old woman. When he reached her, he spoke gently but urgently.

"Excuse me, do you need help? You look like you're having a hard time."

The woman glanced up at him and smiled warmly. "Yes, thank you, young man."

Hezi took the basket from her hands and walked with her until they reached her doorstep.

The old woman gave him a grateful look. "Thank you, really. I appreciate your kindness."

Just as Hezi turned to leave, he paused and gave her a warning.

"Please lock the door behind you, and don't open it for anyone, okay?"

The woman nodded. "I will. Goodbye, and thank you again."

Hezi gave a small wave and walked away, feeling lighter. The weight of his dream no longer hung over him, replaced instead by a sense of satisfaction from the good deed he had done.

***

Hezi arrived quickly at the press office and prepared to head out into the field. Tamar, engrossed in phone calls, was receiving constant updates from witnesses.

"They're organizing a counter-protest," she said, covering the receiver briefly. "You'd better make yourself a coffee. There's time."

Hezi made his way to the kitchenette near the editor's office. Just as he was about to leave with his cup, he bumped into one of the journalists.

"My name is Yaniv," the man introduced himself. "I heard you're working with Tamar."

"Yes," Hezi replied cautiously.

"Just so you know, she always gets what she wants."

"And how is that related to me?" Hezi asked, feeling defensive.

"I've seen the way she looks at you," Yaniv said with a sly grin.

"Really? I have no idea what you're talking about," Hezi responded, feigning ignorance.

Hezi grabbed his coffee and brushed past Yaniv without another word, his mind swirling. The comment unsettled him. Could he be the target Tamar had in mind? He hoped not.

Back at Tamar's desk, Hezi set his coffee on the table and waited patiently for her to finish her phone calls. When they dragged on, he decided to take a walk through the different departments to familiarize himself with their operations. He observed the hustle of the newsroom with interest, occasionally asking questions to staff members who were happy to share their insights.

Eventually, he wandered into the printing house, where the presses were already churning out the next day's papers.

His phone buzzed—it was Tamar.

"Where did you disappear to?" she asked.

"I was just looking around," Hezi answered.

"Get your camera. We're heading out."

Hezi returned to Tamar's desk, where his coffee had gone cold. He gulped it down quickly before grabbing his gear.

On the drive to the protest site, Hezi stared silently out the window, watching the crowded streets blur by. His thoughts drifted to the conversation he dreaded—how and when to tell Tamar he was quitting the job. He feared a confrontation, knowing it could turn ugly.

"Everything okay?" Tamar asked, noticing his silence.

"Yeah, I'm fine," Hezi lied.

She gave him a quick, searching glance but didn't press further.

The drive took longer than expected due to heavy traffic and roadblocks. The radio alternated between upbeat songs and annoying ones, but Hezi tuned them out.

Tamar finally parked on a side street near a shuttered supermarket.

"We need protective gear," she said.

They both put on helmets and vests. Hezi slung his camera equipment over his shoulder, feeling the familiar weight, though his enthusiasm had long since faded.

"Let's go," Tamar ordered.

On the main street, a crowd of Jewish extremists roamed, spoiling for a fight. They targeted any Arab pedestrians they could find, beating them mercilessly.

Hezi, though hardened by years of witnessing violence, felt suffocated by the sheer intensity of the scene. But he kept working, trying to stay focused.

"Get into the crowd and take shots from different angles," Tamar instructed.

This time, Hezi obeyed without hesitation. He positioned himself beside a building and photographed as the rioters stopped a car, dragged the driver out, and beat him brutally.

Meanwhile, Tamar managed to interview some of the aggressors, capturing their rage-fueled justifications. They spoke of revenge, and she probed further, trying to uncover their motivations.

The police eventually arrived, dispersing the mob, though the violence continued sporadically throughout the night. As the hours wore on, the chaos gradually subsided.

Hezi was exhausted—physically and mentally drained from the long day.

"We've got everything we need," Tamar said, for what felt like the hundredth time.

"Take me home," Hezi whispered, almost pleading.

"Why not rest at the hostel?" Tamar suggested.

"No. I have a girlfriend. This thing between us—it can't continue," he said, hoping to put an end to their affair.

"Didn't you enjoy being with me?" she asked with a knowing smile.

Hezi knew any answer would drag him into a conversation he didn't want to have—not now, not ever.

"It was a mistake," he said, gathering his courage. "I'm leaving the job soon."

Tamar's expression darkened. "A mistake? You wanted it just as much as I did!"

Hezi remained silent, knowing that arguing would only make things worse.

"I'm done," he said quietly and started walking up the empty street, leaving her behind.

A few minutes later, Tamar's car pulled up beside him.

"I'm sorry," she said. "You're right. I crossed the line. Let me drive you home—it's too late to be wandering alone."

Hezi hesitated, then relented. He got into the car, and Tamar drove him home without another word.

When he arrived, Keren was fast asleep. Hezi took a shower, scrubbing away the grime of the day and the guilt that clung to him. But sleep didn't come easily. His mind raced, tangled in thoughts of Tamar and how to end things cleanly before they spiraled further out of control. Eventually, exhaustion overtook him, and he drifted off.

He woke in the early afternoon to an empty apartment— Keren was already at work. Hezi shuffled into the kitchen, made himself an omelet with salad, and sat at the table to eat.

Just as he took his first bite, a news report caught his attention. He abandoned his plate and turned up the volume.

The anchor's voice was somber. "A horrifying act of violence against the elderly," she announced.

Hezi's heart sank as the screen displayed the familiar face of the old woman he had helped.

"Unknown assailants broke into her home, assaulted her, and stole her belongings. Police are currently investigating."

Hezi looked surprised. After all, he had explicitly instructed her not to open the door to strangers, yet he couldn't prevent the terrible act. He truly wanted to go to the elderly woman's home to find out what had happened, but upon second thought, he feared the police might suspect him of being the perpetrator, so he decided against it. He felt disappointed, viewing it as a personal failure. Nonetheless, he remained determined to keep trying to save people whenever he had a meaningful dream.

Chapter 20

A week had passed since the riots in the mixed cities, and life seemed to be returning to normal. Yet, in these cities, mistrust lingered between Arab and Jewish neighbors, and the fear of what might happen next was still palpable. Many Jews were boycotting Arab restaurants and businesses in protest of their neighbors' behavior during the unrest. Markets stood empty, and the streets carried a heavy sense of unease.

Hezi was determined to quit his job and take some time off to recuperate. He arrived at the press building to meet with Gideon, walking past Tamar without a word. When he reached Gideon's office, he knocked lightly and asked if he could come in.

Gideon paused his work and gestured for Hezi to sit down.

"I've decided to quit," Hezi said plainly.

Gideon looked surprised. "Can I ask why?"

"The difficult scenes I've witnessed—and the irregular hours—are making it hard to function and live a normal life." Hezi carefully avoided mentioning his relationship with Tamar, hoping to keep things civil.

"We can transfer you to another department—something less stressful. It's a shame to lose you; you're a good employee."

"I'm not sure…" Hezi said, his resolve suddenly wavering.

"Think about it," Gideon urged.

"Okay," Hezi muttered, rising from his seat.

Just as he opened the door, he found Tamar standing right in front of him. Her presence caught him off guard—he hadn't expected her to notice when he passed by earlier.

"Your guy here wants to quit," Gideon remarked with a cynical smile. "I told you before—you've got a knack for driving people away."

"He didn't say anything to me," Tamar responded, feigning innocence.

"Of course, he wouldn't. He's scared of you."

"Am I scary to you?" Tamar asked, turning to Hezi.

"No, you're not. I just need to go now," Hezi replied quickly, wanting to avoid a confrontation. He slipped past them, leaving Tamar and Gideon standing in the doorway, watching him walk away.

When Hezi got home, he exhaled deeply, relieved to be away from the office. He shared the details of his meeting with Gideon with Keren.

"What are you going to do?" she asked.

"Gideon offered me a new role—something less demanding, maybe even more interesting. But... I feel like I really need a break from everything that's happened."

Keren nodded thoughtfully. "Why not just ask for a week off to rest and clear your head before making a decision?"

"That's a good idea."

During his time off, Hezi tried to relax by watching movies, listening to music, and playing video games. But none of these activities gave him real satisfaction. Boredom set in quickly, and he soon felt restless. Needing an outlet, he decided to go out, roaming the streets with his camera, capturing people and unusual moments.

Before long, he found himself wandering through narrow city alleys, drawn toward the elderly woman's house, hoping to get answers about what had happened the day she was attacked.

When he reached her doorstep, he hesitated, worried she might misunderstand his visit and call the police. After a moment, he took a breath and knocked on the door.

A shaky, frightened voice came from inside. "Who's there? I'll call the police!"

"No need," Hezi replied calmly. "I'm the one who helped you carry your bags last week."

There was a pause. Then, the woman peeked through the peephole, her voice still wary. "What do you want?"

"I just wanted to check on you," Hezi said gently.

The elderly woman hesitated but eventually opened the door and let Hezi in, locking it behind him.

Hezi sat down on the sofa while she settled into an armchair across from him.

"Would you like something to drink?" she asked.

"No, thank you," Hezi replied. "Tell me what happened."

"It was early in the evening. The doorbell rang. I remembered you told me not to open the door to strangers, so I asked who it was, just out of curiosity. The man said he was sent by a cable company to fix the infrastructure in my home. Since I've had some trouble with my TV reception, I thought maybe they were here to fix it."

"Did you call the cable company? Report any issues?" Hezi asked.

"No."

"Then why would they show up to fix something?"

"I don't know."

"When I told you not to open the door for anyone, I meant no one."

The elderly woman sighed. "I know... I just wasn't thinking."

Hezi noticed her bruises. "Do you need anything? You're still hurt—it must be painful."

"It's nothing. It'll pass. I don't need anything right now, but thank you."

"Take my number, okay? If you need anything or just want to talk, call me."

"Okay."

"I need to head out now. Don't forget to lock the door after I leave," Hezi reminded her before saying goodbye.

The next day, Hezi's phone rang. He answered quickly, and Officer Itzik's voice came through the line.

"I heard you visited the elderly woman yesterday," the officer said.

Hezi blinked in surprise, not expecting a call from the police.

"Yes, I did."

"You're being summoned to the station today for obstructing an investigation."

"I didn't obstruct anything!"

"You can explain that in the interrogation room."

Hezi's pulse quickened. His mind raced with fear that the police might falsely accuse him of robbing the woman.

"Fine. I'll come," he replied, realizing he had no choice.

Hezi arrived at the station, his heart heavy with anxiety. An officer led him to a side room.

"They're waiting for you in there," the officer said, sounding impatient.

Hezi opened the door and entered. Inside, Officer Itzik sat behind a desk, leafing through some papers.

"Sit down," the officer ordered. Hezi complied.

After a moment, Itzik looked up, locking eyes with Hezi.

"We caught the criminal. You can relax."

Hezi exhaled deeply, relieved.

"But that's not why I called you in," the officer continued. "The elderly woman said you warned her the day before the break-in, told her to lock her door. How did you know?"

"I didn't know anything," Hezi answered, keeping his expression neutral.

"I've told you before—I get the feeling you have a source feeding you information, always getting you to these scenes ahead of us."

"You've said that," Hezi acknowledged, "but you forget—it's my job as a photojournalist to anticipate events and be prepared."

The officer gave him a skeptical look, a hint of amusement flickering in his expression.

"You don't really expect me to believe that, do you? I'm sure there's a more interesting story here."

Hezi kept silent. He had no intention of explaining how he got his information and hoped the officer would drop the matter.

"Can I go now?" Hezi asked.

"You can," the officer replied, leaning back in his chair. "But before you leave, I want to make you an offer."

Hezi raised an eyebrow. "An offer?"

"I want you to join us in a new department—'Cold Cases.'"

"What does that involve?"

"Solving complex cases: missing persons who were never found, old murder cases with no leads."

"I don't have experience in that field," Hezi pointed out.

"True, but you've got sharp instincts. You could be valuable. No pressure—just think about it. The pay's good, and there's room for advancement."

Chapter 21

Keren came home from work exhausted and went straight to the shower to refresh herself. When she came out, Hezi told her about his meeting with the police and the intriguing offer he had received.

"I think it's worse than the job you already have, but it's your decision," she said.

"Yes, you're right. 'One is no better than the other.' I think I'll quit and stay home until I find a more relaxed job in a less stressful environment."

"And what will you do at home all day?" she asked.

"I'll keep taking photos in the streets."

"And what about your income?"

"I need to relax first."

"You know what? Since you're already taking pictures, maybe you should hold your own exhibition."

"An exhibition... That's a great idea. How did I not think of that before?" he mumbled to himself.

The next morning, Hezi called Gideon and informed him of his decision. He was determined to leave journalism and start a new chapter in his life.

"I'm sorry to hear that. Let me know if you change your mind," Gideon said.

"Okay," Hezi replied, hanging up. A wave of relief washed over him.

Over the following days, Hezi focused on sorting through the photos he had taken so far, trying to select the best ones—a daunting task, as most were exceptional. He spent hours in front of the computer, scanning through image after image, searching for the perfect shots.

Suddenly, his phone rang. It was Tamar, urging him to return to work. She promised to behave more respectfully and considerately. Hezi told her he had already made up his mind and wasn't planning to change it.

Tamar persisted, pleading with him to reconsider. At one point, his patience snapped. "I'm going to hang up now," he warned.

Just before he disconnected the call, Tamar's voice came through: "You can't just leave like that—you'll hear from me again."

And she kept her word. Tamar called several times a day. At first, Hezi answered, repeating the same explanations over and over. But as the days passed, his patience wore thin. He began checking the caller ID and hanging up as soon as he saw her name.

Eventually, the calls stopped. Tamar gave up, and Hezi breathed a sigh of relief.

Hezi finalized the selection for his first photo collection. The competition between the images was fierce—each photo told a unique story. Limited to just fifty photos, Hezi struggled to narrow them down. Occasionally, he turned to Keren for her input when he couldn't decide.

One afternoon, around five o'clock, Hezi went out to buy groceries at the local supermarket. When he returned, bags full of food in hand, he opened the door—and froze.

There, sitting on the living room sofa, was Tamar, engaged in a lively conversation with Keren. His heart skipped a beat, and his face turned pale.

Their conversation was cheerful and friendly. Hezi took a moment to gather himself, then entered the room and placed the grocery bags near the refrigerator. Slowly, he approached them.

"Hezi, meet our new neighbor—Tamar," Keren said with a bright smile.

Hezi struggled to maintain composure, acting as if he had never met Tamar before.

"Nice to meet you," he said, forcing a smile and avoiding her gaze.

Tamar grinned. "It seems we have a few things in common."

"Really," Hezi said, his voice strained, feeling as though his worst nightmare was coming true.

"We both love shopping for clothes and watching thrillers."

Hezi thought to himself that their encounter felt like a scene from a horror movie—one that only got more complicated as it progressed—and he feared it would end in tragedy.

"I think I'll go now," Tamar said.

"Okay, keep in touch," Keren replied.

Hezi muttered inwardly, "That's just what I need—for them to keep in touch."

Tamar rose from the sofa, glanced at Hezi, and said in a calm tone, "Nice to meet you." Then, she walked to the door, opened it, and left.

"I suggest you stay away from her," Hezi said firmly.

"Why? She seems nice," Keren responded.

"That's exactly the problem with people like her. They always hide something. Who knows?"

"Oh, come on, there's no reason to be so suspicious," Keren said dismissively.

"Listen to me. I have a bad feeling about her," he insisted.

But Keren remained unmoved, brushing off his concern.

Hezi looked at her, feeling helpless.

Trying to tell Keren the truth felt like the worst possible option—one that would almost certainly lead to a painful, messy breakup. For now, he decided to focus on the photo exhibition. Afterward, he would figure out what to do about the situation.

The next day, Hezi met with Moshe, the director of the local art museum, to discuss the exhibition. He arrived on time, carrying a large bag filled with the best photos he had taken and carefully developed.

He entered the museum, excitement bubbling inside him. After a brief inspection, the security guard directed him to Moshe's office.

"Nice to meet you," Moshe said warmly, shaking Hezi's hand. "Please, have a seat."

Hezi introduced himself, sharing his background and the experience he had gained as a photojournalist.

"Let's see your photos," Moshe said.

Hezi eagerly spread several large prints across the desk, explaining where and under what circumstances each photo was taken.

Moshe studied the images carefully and was visibly impressed. "These are excellent," he said, nodding thoughtfully. "We'll schedule the exhibition in about two weeks."

Then, Moshe took Hezi on a tour of the museum. As they walked through one of the exhibition halls, Moshe pointed to a wall.

"Your photos will be displayed here," he said.

Hezi felt a surge of satisfaction.

"You'll be responsible for promoting the exhibition and managing it," Moshe added.

"Understood," Hezi replied, shaking Moshe's hand before saying goodbye.

When Hezi returned home, he found the house empty. A note, held by a magnet on the refrigerator, caught his eye. It read: "Went to the mall with Tamar to buy clothes, will be back later."

Hezi's blood boiled. His frustration reached a breaking point. "This has gone too far," he thought bitterly. "I need to put an end to this."

He feared that the truth about his connection to Tamar would come out—and that he would pay dearly for it. The only way to prevent disaster was to confront her directly and convince her to stay silent.

He knew he needed to find the right moment to meet with Tamar privately—at her home—where they could settle things once and for all.

***

One evening, Hezi gathered his courage and decided to confront Tamar at her apartment. He stood at her door, heart pounding, with a lingering fear that his efforts would be futile—that he would leave empty-handed.

Worse still, he feared the encounter might take a turn for the worse. What if she decided to take revenge in the ugliest and most painful way imaginable?

He rang the doorbell, and in that moment, every instinct told him to run—but his feet stayed rooted to the spot. He braced himself, imagining Tamar insulting him and slamming the door in his face.

After a brief pause, the door opened, and to his surprise, Tamar stood there wearing a red bathrobe, sloppily tied around her.

"May I come in?" he asked.

"Of course," she replied, stepping aside without further comment.

Hezi entered and stood awkwardly in the center of the living room while Tamar closed the door behind him. He glanced around the apartment; several boxes remained unpacked, adding to the unsettling feeling that she wasn't yet fully settled—or planning to stay long.

"We need to talk," he said quietly.

"Would you like something to drink? Maybe a fruit smoothie?" she asked with a smile.

"No, thank you."

"I'm making one for myself anyway," she said lightly.

"I'll pass."

"Suit yourself," she shrugged, disappearing into the kitchen. Soon, the sound of a blender whirred as she mixed oranges, bananas, and pineapple.

When she returned with her smoothie, she asked, "Would you like to sit?"

"No, I'll stand."

Hezi took a breath and said, "I need you to leave Keren alone. She hasn't done anything to you. There's no reason for her to get hurt."

Tamar smirked, her expression teasing. "I think Keren enjoys my company. Why would I hurt her?" she said, feigning innocence.

"Our relationship is over. You need to move on with your life," Hezi said firmly.

Tamar fixed her gaze on him, amused. "Move on? Do you think I'm some disposable thing you can toss aside when you're done? No, Hezi. You need to take responsibility for what you've done."

Hezi's temper flared. "What responsibility? You were the one who seduced me, remember?"

"And you didn't resist," Tamar said coldly, her expression darkening.

"As if resisting would've made a difference," Hezi snapped. "I'm warning you—stay away from us."

"Or what?" she challenged; her tone defiant.

"Or you'll regret it," Hezi muttered, storming toward the door. He yanked it open and slammed it shut behind him.

His heart pounded furiously as he walked away, frustration bubbling inside him. The conversation had gone worse than he'd expected. He feared Tamar would soon try to come between him and Keren—it felt like only a matter of time. He had tried everything he could think of, and yet he had no solution in sight. He had to keep his past with Tamar hidden at all costs.

That night, Hezi had another dream—a particularly disturbing one. In it, he saw a young girl crossing the park at dusk, only to be ambushed by an older man lurking in the bushes. The man dragged her into the undergrowth and assaulted her.

Hezi woke up in a cold sweat, her desperate cries for help still echoing in his mind. He quickly grabbed a piece of paper from the nightstand and jotted down every detail he could remember— the park, the girl, and the attacker. Every piece of information might be crucial.

The next evening, Hezi decided to go to the park near his home. He sat on a bench, watching the passersby, hoping to spot something out of the ordinary. People strolled along the paths or sat on benches, chatting quietly. Everything seemed normal.

As night began to fall, the park emptied, and Hezi found himself alone in a secluded corner, bored and questioning whether the dream had been nothing more than a figment of his imagination.

Just then, a young girl appeared, crossing the path as if on her way home. Moments later, Hezi noticed a strange man emerging from a distant trail. Alarmed, Hezi jumped from the bench and hurried toward the girl.

When he reached her, he blocked her path.

"It's not safe to go this way," he warned. "There's dangerous activity in the park—criminals. You should turn back and take a different route."

The girl looked at him uncertainly, but something in his tone convinced her. She nodded and turned around, heading out of the park.

Hezi scanned the area, but the strange man had vanished. Relieved, he exhaled deeply, thankful he had intervened in time.

Determined to make sure he hadn't missed anything, Hezi returned to the park the following evening. He arrived early and waited for hours, sitting on the same bench, his eyes darting around for any signs of trouble.

But nothing unusual happened. The girl from the previous night didn't appear, and the strange man was nowhere to be seen. Satisfied that the threat had passed, Hezi finally returned home, feeling at ease.

***

A week before the exhibition was set to open, Hezi arrived at the museum, bringing the best photos he had taken, framed and ready for display. After a thorough inspection, the guard opened the glass door, allowed him to enter, and wished him good luck.

Hezi was filled with excitement as he reached the space Moshe had allocated for him. Standing in the center, he gazed at the bare wall. He closed his eyes, trying to envision the arrangement of the photos. When he opened them again, he laid the photos on the floor, organizing them into groups by theme.

Once satisfied with the arrangement, he began lifting the photos from the floor and hanging them on the wall. After he finished, he called Moshe to get his opinion on the exhibition he had prepared. Moshe arrived and was impressed.

Hezi took out his camera and photographed the exhibition from several angles. When he got home, he shared the photos on social media, adding details about the location and the date of the exhibition's opening.

Late in the evening, he settled down on the sofa and turned on the TV to watch a comedy show. Suddenly, the broadcast was interrupted by a news flash, and a somber news anchor reported the rape of a young girl in the park. The suspect had been arrested, and his detention had been extended.

Despite knowing about the incident in advance, Hezi felt powerless to prevent it. He was left disappointed and disheartened.

Chapter 22

Hezi was excited about the opening event of his photography exhibition. He dressed in especially festive clothes and wore the new shoes he had bought just for the occasion. He didn't wear a tie to avoid looking too formal. The event was scheduled to begin at eight in the evening.

Hezi arrived with Keren about half an hour early to ensure everything was in order and to greet the visitors. The first guests arrived, entered, and began wandering around the exhibition space, admiring the photographs. Hezi mingled with them, introduced himself, and explained the meaning behind some of the photos. As more people arrived, the room filled with energy, though eventually, the flow of visitors slowed. Hezi felt satisfied as he looked around, seeing so many people interested in his work. He turned to Keren and expressed his happiness.

Around ten o'clock, a surprising and unexpected figure arrived—it was Itzik, the police officer, now in civilian clothes. He wandered through the exhibition, examining the photographs on the walls. Then he approached Hezi, who was speaking with one of the visitors, and whispered, "Very impressive."

Hezi turned to him and thanked him.

"Can you spare a moment for a quick one-on-one conversation?" Itzik asked.

Hezi glanced around, making sure Keren wasn't watching.

"Let's step outside," he finally said.

Once outside the museum, Itzik got straight to the point. "About a week ago, a brutal rape occurred in the park. The victim told the police that a few days prior, a stranger had approached her and warned her not to go to a certain place. She described the stranger, and the description matches you."

"There are plenty of people who fit my description," Hezi said, trying to defend himself.

"We have security cameras in the park."

Hezi fell silent. There was no point in arguing if the police had solid proof.

"Relax, the rapist has already been caught," Itzik continued. "I'm here to ask how you knew. And don't tell me it was just a coincidence."

"I have dreams. I can't control them. They're... prophetic, in a way."

"I figured as much. Warning the victim in advance won't stop the crime; it will happen anyway. But if you track the attacker, there's a chance you could stop it in real time."

"I didn't think of that, but I don't have the physical ability to confront an attacker. He'd overpower me."

"You don't need to confront him—that's our job. So, what have you decided? Will you join us?"

Hezi paused, considering his answer carefully.

"I'll agree on one condition," he finally said. "There's someone bothering me who won't leave me alone. If you can get her away from me, I'll join."

"That might be tricky. We only handle criminal matters like theft, murder, sexual harassment. But romantic relationships..."

Hezi looked disappointed. "What if I claim sexual harassment?" he asked, hoping it might offer a solution.

"You can file a complaint, but if it goes to trial, you'll need evidence. If she accuses you of harassment—even if it's false—you'll be in trouble because the judges might side with her."

"So, there's nothing that can be done?" he asked, clearly frustrated.

"What's so bad about being loved?"

"I already have a girlfriend whom I love."

"Then tell her the truth—isn't that simpler?"

"I tried. It didn't work. Now she's hanging out with my girlfriend, following her to different places. Who knows what she's planning? Some kind of twisted revenge."

Itzik seemed amused by the idea of a love triangle.

"I'll tell you what. Join the police, and we'll figure out a solution together to handle this problem."

"Alright," Hezi finally agreed. "I need to get back inside before my girlfriend notices I'm gone and starts asking questions."

Itzik bid him goodbye and went on his way.

Hezi re-entered the exhibition, feeling dejected as he weaved through the guests until he reached Keren, who stood by one of the photos.

"So, what do you think of the exhibition?" he asked, forcing a smile, trying to mask his concern.

"There's no doubt—you're very talented," she replied.

While speaking with Keren, Hezi noticed Tamar out of the corner of his eye. She had just walked in, dressed elegantly, her outfit flattering her figure. Her entrance caused a few guests to glance her way with curiosity.

"I don't remember inviting her," he whispered to Keren.

"I did," she said.

Hezi felt his world crumble. He wanted to vanish, to sink into the ground and disappear. But there was no escape, no hiding. It felt as though he was standing naked under a glaring spotlight. His heart pounded, each beat thudding in his chest as though it might burst. He tried to calm his breathing but to no avail.

Tamar approached with a warm smile, her blonde hair pulled back and subtly scented with fragrant oil. She went straight to Keren, embracing her warmly, then turned and shook Hezi's hand, as if maintaining a semblance of polite distance.

Tamar looked back at Keren. "Maybe you could show me Hezi's wonderful photographs?" she asked, as if Hezi wasn't standing there, as if she knew nothing of his work.

"Of course," Keren replied with a smile. The two women linked arms and walked toward one of the photo-adorned walls.

Hezi stood there alone, his anger and jealousy surging as he watched them slowly drift away.

At that moment, he resolved to find a way to end this, no matter the cost.

The time Moshe had allocated for Hezi's exhibition was drawing to a close. The guests and occasional visitors who had wandered in out of curiosity began to leave, one by one. The hall gradually emptied.

Hezi walked over to Keren and told her it was time to go. He had already arranged with Moshe to return the next day to collect the photographs he'd displayed.

"Are you coming?" he urged, as she was deep in conversation with Tamar.

"In a moment," she said, still absorbed in the conversation, seemingly ignoring Hezi's presence. When they finally wrapped up, Keren agreed to leave.

"Do you need a ride?" she asked Tamar.

"No, thanks. I drove myself," Tamar replied.

Hezi breathed a sigh of relief. The last thing he needed was to drive her and listen to her the entire way home.

The three of them left the hall together.

"The exhibition was fascinating," Tamar said to Hezi. "It's clear you have talent."

She then bid them farewell and walked toward her car. Hezi and Keren headed to their car and drove home.

***

Hezi was apprehensive about his upcoming job interview at the local police station. He feared that the experiences he'd face there might worsen his condition, but he had no choice. He needed Tamar out of his life before things got worse, and this seemed like the only solution.

Hezi dressed in his best clothes, checked himself in the mirror to ensure his appearance was flawless, shaved, and combed his hair.

At the entrance of the police station, Itzik was waiting for him. Spotting him, Itzik smiled and said, "Come on, they're waiting for us in the office. Show confidence, and everything will go smoothly."

Hezi, looking tense, tried to mask his unease.

When they reached the office door, Itzik introduced him. "Meet Kobi, in charge of recruitment for the organization."

"Come in," Kobi invited, and Hezi entered, sitting across from him.

Itzik waited outside as the door closed.

The interview lasted about twenty minutes, during which Hezi was asked about his previous jobs.

Hezi mentioned two places where he had worked, explaining his role in each.

"We're looking for someone with sharp instincts and creative thinking, and you seem to fit the bill," Kobi said.

"What position are we talking about?" Hezi asked, though Itzik had already given him a brief explanation outside the museum.

"The homicide division. You'll undergo detective training, and once completed, you'll get your own office and work on cold cases that have been unsolved for years. It's a serious, complex challenge."

Hezi hesitated, fear gnawing at him—could he meet the demands? He had no prior experience in this field, coming from a completely different background.

"Itzik will mentor you during the onboarding process," Kobi added. "What do you think?"

"I agree. I'll do my best," Hezi replied.

"Great. Open the door and let Itzik in."

Hezi did as instructed.

"We just need to finalize the terms of employment. You'll need to sign a few documents, mostly confidentiality agreements."

After Hezi filled in the required details, Itzik accompanied him to continue the process.

Later, Hezi returned home, eager to tell Keren about the job and the procedures he'd gone through. But as he stepped inside, he only managed, "I was at the police station today to..." before noticing Tamar sitting at the dining table, deep in conversation with Keren. His face fell, and he fell silent.

"What were you going to say?" Keren asked.

"I got a job at the police department," he replied.

"In what role?" Tamar chimed in.

"Solving murder cases," he answered.

"Really?" Tamar seemed genuinely surprised, not expecting him to go this far. But once she composed herself, she saw potential. "We could work together—you as a detective, and me as a crime journalist."

The last thing I need, Hezi thought. He forced a smile, said nothing, and headed to take a shower.

Hezi started his first day of work with determination. Itzik was waiting for him at the entrance.

"The course will begin in about a week," Itzik explained. "For now, I'll show you your office. Get settled in, and later I'll take you to the supply room for your uniform and badge."

Hezi sat at his desk, feeling bored, hoping something exciting would happen soon—but it didn't. After two hours, Itzik finally entered his office.

"You look down. Still thinking about that woman?" Itzik asked. "Listen, if she wanted to hurt you, she could've done it by now. Maybe she just wants to be close to you."

"No, I'm certain she's planning something. I have a feeling I'll hear from her soon."

"I think your fear's unfounded. But come on, we've been assigned to visit malls and stores to enforce mask mandates and social distancing."

Hezi looked at him in disbelief—this was not what he had joined the police for.

"There's a manpower shortage, and we've been recruited for the task."

They headed to the supply room. Hezi received his new uniform and badge, changed in the locker room, and when he emerged, Itzik said, "No doubt, the uniform suits you."

They left the station, got into a police car, and headed to a mall. Hezi found himself chasing after shoppers, urging them to wear masks. Sometimes he succeeded, other times not, and some even got fined for refusal. It was a frustrating, exhausting day, and he hoped it wouldn't become routine. But over the following days, he found himself patrolling shopping centers repeatedly.

A week passed, and the detective course began. Hezi arrived at the police academy, focused on his goal. He worried the course would require him to stay at the academy during the week, only returning home on weekends. He didn't like sleeping away from home, although he had done so occasionally in his previous job. His biggest concern was that Tamar would exploit his absence to turn Keren against him. But he had no choice—he had to suppress the thought for now.

At the residential area, an officer checked the list of participants, recognized Hezi's name, and gave him his room number. Hezi entered and found his roommate, Yogev. They introduced themselves, and Hezi, exhausted, lay down on his bed.

Later, they gathered in a large hall. The lecturer, Doron, entered with a slight delay. A large police emblem hung on the wall behind him.

"Welcome," he began. "I'm Doron. This course will cover the role's perception and provide you with tools to act professionally and legally in the situations you'll encounter. By the end, you'll be experts in operational intelligence and detective work—surveillance, tracking, stakeouts, arrests, searches, and protecting individuals in distress. Any questions so far?"

The officers remained silent.

Doron looked around, expecting a raised hand. When none appeared, he said, "I'll start with a video about detective work, then there will be a break. After that, we'll dive into the course."

The lights dimmed, and Hezi watched the half-hour promotional video with great interest. Afterward, he joined the others for a break.

Once the break ended, Hezi returned to the hall. The first slide displayed on the wall showed a gruesome crime scene.

"Can anyone tell us what we're seeing?" Doron asked.

One officer replied, "A woman lying on the floor, drenched in blood."

"Anyone else?" Doron asked.

Hezi raised his hand.

"Yes, go ahead."

"I see footprints, a torn curtain, and a broken window. I assume that's where the attacker fled."

"Excellent," Doron praised. "That's exactly what I expect— scan the scene and look for suspicious clues. Avoid assumptions and examine every possibility."

The next slide showed findings from various murder scenes.

In the third slide, a note appeared.

"Can anyone tell me what they see?"

"A suicide note," one officer blurted out.

Hezi raised his hand again.

"Yes?"

"The handwriting is too neat. A suicide note is usually written in haste."

"So?"

"It might be fabricated."

"Well done," Doron nodded. "That's the level of thoroughness I expect."

At the end of the day, Hezi returned to his room, pleased with the compliments from the lecturer. He later called Keren to tell her about his day, and she was happy to hear from him.

Chapter 23

A new government was sworn in after four rounds of elections. The coalition was made up of parties with differing, even opposing, ideologies. Some doubted it would last, but despite many predictions, it held together and functioned well.

Hezi watched the swearing-in ceremony on TV, secretly hoping that long-neglected issues, particularly in the healthcare and education systems, would finally be addressed and improved.

***

The course ended after a grueling month. Hezi was among the top-performing officers, excelling both theoretically and practically. Given his achievements, he expected to be assigned to a particularly challenging role. However, he was disappointed when his superiors decided he should first join an observation team, whose job was to alert field forces in real time about dangerous criminals during their activities.

Hezi returned to his gloomy office, bracing for another dull day. Suddenly, Itzik entered without knocking, sat down in the chair across from him, uninvited.

"How was the course?" Itzik asked with a grin.

"Fascinating," Hezi replied curtly.

"Ready for your first mission?"

Hezi stared at him for a moment, dreading another tedious assignment. Reluctantly, he agreed.

"There's a big drug deal going down. We need to observe and report to the field forces."

"Do I need a weapon?" Hezi asked.

"No. We'll just be sitting in a car, watching."

"Okay," Hezi said, standing up.

Hezi got into an unmarked car and sat next to Itzik. In the back seat were two other people he didn't know, dressed in civilian clothes and heavily armed.

Itzik started the car, and they sped through the crowded streets. Hezi was surprised that such an operation was happening in broad daylight, right in front of everyone. Normally, these kinds of things went down late at night to preserve the element of surprise.

But since he didn't know the reasoning, he stayed quiet, keeping alert for what was to come.

The car entered an industrial area and stopped near a building still under construction. The two officers in the back got out and disappeared into a nearby alley.

Fifteen minutes later, two more civilian cars arrived, parking close by. Stern-faced officers in plain clothes stepped out, armed and taking up cover positions around the area.

Itzik patted Hezi on the shoulder. "You look tense. It's fine. You're allowed to be."

He handed Hezi a pair of binoculars, keeping one for himself. "Look at the building with the blue metal door," he instructed.

An hour passed, and nothing happened. Hezi felt like they were wasting time. Then, suddenly, a sleek black car appeared, parking near the metal door. A woman in her twenties got out, wearing a blue dress and black sunglasses. She walked up to the door and knocked five times in a specific rhythm.

The door opened, and a bald, suspicious-looking man stepped out. He glanced around, scanning for danger. Finding none, he gestured for her to come inside.

Itzik reported the situation to the field forces and instructed them to prepare for the raid.

"That woman is an undercover cop," Itzik told Hezi. "When she gives the signal, we storm in."

"And if the signal doesn't come?" Hezi asked, concerned.

"We've got twenty minutes. If no signal comes by then, we go in anyway."

"And that could mean casualties, possibly including the undercover cop," Hezi said.

"These officers are skilled, experienced in situations like this. They'll recognize her in time and neutralize the threats," Itzik assured him.

Hezi hoped the situation would end peacefully.

Minutes passed in a blur. Suddenly, Itzik received the signal. He ordered the forces to move in.

Officers gathered at the door while others provided cover. Some surrounded the building, taking up firing positions. Two officers arrived with tools and broke down the door. The entry team stormed in, and after a brief shootout, silence fell.

"Let's move," Itzik ordered.

Hezi and Itzik exited the car, advancing toward the entrance. Itzik, more alert than ever, drew his gun.

As they approached, drug dealers—now handcuffed—were being escorted out by officers, one by one.

Inside the building, the undercover officer greeted them.

"You did a great job," Itzik complimented her.

"Thanks," she replied, stepping outside to catch her breath.

"Her name's Osherit," Itzik explained. "She's been on these guys for a while. They thought she was buying for personal use. She had to bring real money to make it convincing."

They wandered around the hall, impressed by the amount of drugs seized. Itzik struck up a conversation with another officer while Hezi continued exploring.

At the far end of the hall, Hezi found a small room. Inside were a bed, a fridge, a bathroom, a tiny kitchen, and a board hanging on the wall.

Hezi approached the board and saw instructions for growing plants: light levels, oxygen requirements, food quantities, watering schedules, temperature control, and more. He figured they were for growing cannabis.

Itzik entered the room. "What did you find?"

"This looks like a cannabis growing lab. We need to locate it."

Hezi scanned the floor and noticed a wooden plank in a corner. He lifted it, revealing a lit shaft with a ladder leading down.

"Wait," Itzik said before stepping out to call for backup. When he returned, he said, "We've got officers coming to secure us while we head down."

Gun drawn, Itzik descended the ladder first, followed by two officers, with Hezi bringing up the rear.

They found themselves in a large underground chamber, dimly lit. The air was thick with the strong smell of cannabis.

Rows of tall plants grew under specialized lights, supported by a computerized irrigation system.

Itzik reported the discovery to Superintendent Beniso, and additional forces were dispatched to secure the site.

Hezi climbed back up for some air, noticing officers gathering, curious about the find. He was heading toward the exit when he suddenly spotted Tamar arriving with a camera crew. His face went pale.

"What are you doing here?" he asked uneasily.

Tamar stood in front of him, smug. "The police spokesperson invited us to cover the event," she said, her tone half-reproachful as she poked a finger into his chest. "You might want to adjust your attitude toward me. It wouldn't hurt to cooperate. After all, we share a little secret, remember?" With that, she walked away.

Hezi stood there, stunned, watching her leave. He then stepped outside, standing by the car they'd arrived in, breathing in the fresh air and wishing the media circus would end quickly. All he wanted was to go home, take a shower, and maybe catch a nap.

Chapter 24

Hezi expected a quiet, peaceful evening. Watching the news, he sighed. It seemed like there was never a dull or comforting moment—only disasters and constant trouble. This time, the headlines were about incendiary balloons launched from Gaza. Fields around the Gaza Strip were ablaze. Firefighters were rushing from one fire to the next, battling flames that devoured crops and left behind scorched earth. Farmers, who had lost everything, appeared on the screen, pleading with the government to stop the destruction.

Hezi didn't want to watch those scenes anymore. He turned off the TV and decided to go to bed. Just as he was about to fall asleep, the phone rang. Exhausted, Hezi got out of bed to answer. It was Itzik on the other end.

"I hope I'm not disturbing you," Itzik said.

"You're not," Hezi lied.

"I have some good news. Tomorrow, there's a ceremony at the station. They're giving you a certificate of appreciation for uncovering the drug lab. This means you'll soon be doing the job you were trained for."

"Great. See you tomorrow," Hezi replied, ending the call before heading back to bed.

That night, he had another dream. In it, he saw a man walking down the street when a shootout suddenly erupted. The man was hit by a stray bullet, collapsed, and died on the spot. Hezi woke up in a panic, sat up, and quickly jotted down the details. He lay back down but struggled to sleep. Glancing to the side, he saw Keren sleeping peacefully, her back turned to him. Hezi felt a hug would comfort him, but he didn't want to wake her. He stared at the ceiling for a long time before finally drifting off again.

The next day, after the emotional ceremony where Hezi received the certificate of appreciation, he approached Itzik. "Can I talk to you privately?" he asked.

"Sure."

The two stepped away from the group and stood at the edge of the courtyard.

"I had a dream about a murder that will happen tonight."

"You know we can't allocate manpower based on a dream. This is an investigation we'll have to conduct ourselves, without anyone knowing."

"You're right."

"I'll pick you up in the squad car this evening. In the meantime, try to figure out where the event will take place so we don't waste time wandering aimlessly."

"Alright."

At 7:00 p.m., the two arrived in the squad car on a main street in the southern part of the city.

"I'm sure it's here. All the signs point to it," Hezi said to Itzik.

"We'll wait in the car."

Pedestrians walked back and forth on the sidewalk without interruption. The two waited for over an hour and were almost ready to give up when suddenly a masked man on a motorcycle emerged from a nearby alley and began shooting at a man who had just left one of the busy restaurants. Itzik grabbed his radio, reported the incident to the station, and called for backup. He then jumped out of the car with his gun drawn and ran toward the scene while Hezi stayed in place, watching through the windshield.

The man who had left the restaurant was shot at close range, collapsed, and fell to the ground, bleeding. Another passerby, who had accidentally stumbled into the area, was also shot and severely injured. Hezi called the station to report the situation and urgently requested an ambulance. The motorcyclist quickly fled the scene and disappeared.

Ten minutes later, which felt like an eternity, two police cars and an ambulance arrived. Two paramedics rushed out with a stretcher, placed the injured men on it, loaded them into the ambulance, and sped away with sirens blaring.

Itzik looked disappointed. The event had ended so quickly that he hadn't had a chance to react and catch the shooter. The police cleared the curious onlookers from the area and began collecting witness statements. Itzik returned to the squad car, sat down, and remained silent, trying to process what had just happened.

"I told you it was hopeless," Hezi said in frustration.

Itzik looked at him for a moment before replying, "We'll learn from this for next time." Then he added, "I'll take you home. Tomorrow, we'll get more details about the event. Maybe they'll track down the motorcyclist and catch him; who knows?"

Itzik dropped Hezi off at home and continued on his way. At the elevator, Hezi ran into Tamar. He sighed, realizing he'd have to engage in a conversation he didn't want and provide explanations.

"Do you have something for me?" she asked, looking serious.

"It's under police investigation; I can't share details right now."

"Something general," she pressed.

"A shooting incident in the south of the city. A masked man on a motorcycle shot someone coming out of a restaurant."

"Any fatalities?"

"I don't know yet. It seems there are serious injuries."

"See, when you want to cooperate, you can. It's not that hard," she said, stepping into the elevator.

Hezi didn't want to ride up with her, so he waited for the next elevator to arrive.

When Keren opened the door, Hezi walked in, and she asked how his day had been. He briefly replied, without going into detail, "Exhausting."

Keren suggested they go for a walk to unwind, and Hezi happily agreed. Some fresh air would do him good. The air was cool, and moonlight peeked through the clouds, casting a soft glow on the busy streets. They weren't walking alone; other couples were following the same path. The walk in the open air worked wonders, and Hezi felt much better. They reminisced about old memories, and Hezi felt lucky that Keren had stood by him and continued to do so, even during tough times.

When they returned home, they had dinner and sat down to watch a comedy together. Keren rested her head on his shoulder, and Hezi held her hand, knowing he must protect this precious relationship at all costs. But what was the red line he would never cross? When would the moment come when he'd have no choice but to tell her the truth, regardless of the heavy price he'd pay? Only time would tell.

The next day, when Hezi arrived at the office, he saw Itzik waiting for him on a chair, looking tense.

"What's going on?" Hezi asked, placing his bag on a chair.

"We still haven't tracked down the assassin on the motorcycle. The guy who left the restaurant died from his injuries in the hospital. The other guy, the passerby who was accidentally caught in the crossfire, is still in critical condition and on a ventilator."

"Let's hope he recovers soon," Hezi replied.

"There'll be an inquiry about the event. They'll ask questions like: what were we doing there exactly? Don't worry; it's a routine process. Just say I took you home and that we stopped to pick something up along the way. We'll make something up."

"Alright," Hezi agreed, reluctantly.

"Don't forget," she said and hung up.

***

The next morning, Hezi arrived at the police station, expecting a quiet, calm day. On his desk lay the first folder of an unsolved case. He placed his bag down, made a cup of coffee, and returned to his office. Sitting in his chair, he stared at the folder, hesitating to open it and face the gruesome horrors inside.

Itzik entered Hezi's office, looked at him, and asked, "Aren't you curious to open it?"

"Let me finish my coffee first," Hezi replied.

"Take your time, no rush. Then update me on your thoughts about the case," Itzik said before leaving.

Hezi slowly sipped his coffee, staring at the folder as if mesmerized, contemplating the disturbing images he was about to witness. When he finally finished his coffee, he opened the folder and wasn't surprised. Inside was a set of laminated photos showing the body of a young girl lying lifeless in an abandoned field, marked by signs of violence. There were also photos of evidence collected from the scene.

Hezi removed the photos from their plastic sleeves, spread them across the table, and examined them carefully. He then read the autopsy report, sighed, stood up, and walked to Itzik's office.

"There's information missing," Hezi said.

"Exactly. That's your job," Itzik replied with a smile.

"I need to go to the scene of the crime. Where is it?"

"In a forest near the city of Ramla. I'll take you there in about an hour if you want."

"Okay," Hezi replied, leaving the office.

About an hour later, Itzik returned to Hezi's office. "Ready?"

"Yeah."

The two left the station and drove to an abandoned forest on the outskirts of the city. Itzik navigated a dirt road full of potholes until he reached a bend and pulled over to the side of the road.

"We're here," he said, opening the door and stepping outside. Hezi followed, carrying a small suitcase containing the case file and investigative tools.

They entered the forest, and Itzik stopped near one of the trees. "This is the scene. This is where the body was found."

Itzik sat down on one of the rocks while Hezi opened the suitcase, pulled out the folder, and examined the photos, trying to match the camera angles with the evidence in the field. He then took out a special camera, plastic bags, and tweezers, walking through the forest in search of additional clues that may have been missed. Suddenly, he found strands of hair, a piece of fabric, and faint footprints in the mud. He collected the evidence, placed it in plastic bags, and documented the footprints with his camera.

"I think I've got what I need," he declared.

On the way back to the patrol car, he noticed drops of blood on one of the rocks and took a picture of them as well. He used a swab to scrape a drop of blood from the rock, put it in a bag, and sealed it. He also noticed drag marks and documented them with his camera.

When he finished, he returned to Itzik.

"So, did you find anything new?" Itzik asked.

"I found some interesting evidence. It needs to be tested in the forensics lab."

Hezi was silent, staring into the distance with a focused gaze. "What's that building over there?" he asked, pointing.

"That's a cardboard factory," came the reply.

"Let's go there. Maybe they have security cameras, and we can find footage of the incident. We'll ask them if they've seen any suspicious people around."

"Alright."

The two got into the patrol car and drove to the nearby industrial area. When they arrived, they showed their police badges at the entrance, requested to meet the manager, and were granted permission.

"How can I help you?" asked Menashe, the manager, who appeared both surprised and somewhat anxious about the unexpected visit.

"There was a murder in the forest near here about two weeks ago. Did you see or hear anything?" Itzik asked.

"No. As you know, this is just a factory," he replied.

"Can we check the footage from the security cameras?" Hezi asked.

"Of course. Please wait here, and I'll bring it to you."

Twenty minutes later, Menashe returned with the footage. Hezi took the recordings from him and placed them in his bag. "We'll review them, and when we're done, we'll return them."

"Sure, whatever you need."

Itzik and Hezi said their goodbyes and returned to the police station. Once there, Hezi quickly handed over the evidence for lab analysis. Then he went with Itzik to the computer room and gave the security footage to Liran, the technician.

Liran played the video on the computer screen at Hezi's request, reviewing about two hours of footage for unusual activity.

"Rewind more. It happened more than two weeks ago," Hezi instructed.

"Stop!" Hezi suddenly shouted when he noticed something unclear. "Rewind a bit."

"Stop! Freeze the frame," he ordered.

Hezi leaned closer to the screen, and Itzik joined him. "Do you see that? Zoom in," he asked Liran after spotting a black figure getting out of a car in the forest, followed by a girl.

"It's an older man. Try zooming in more to get a clearer look at his face."

Liran tried, but due to the distance, the face appeared blurry.

"Print the picture. Let's go to the victim's family to gather more evidence," he said to Itzik.

"We already did that. Didn't you read the report?" Itzik responded dismissively.

"Let's go again; we're missing details."

Reluctantly, Itzik joined Hezi, not expecting to uncover anything new.

The two arrived at the victim's home, introduced themselves, and went inside. Hezi wanted to learn more about the girl—her lifestyle, her history, what bothered or troubled her, and whether she had enemies. He discovered some interesting facts: the girl had previously been hospitalized in a hostel for at-risk youth and had dropped out of several schools.

Hezi entered her room, which appeared ordinary. He asked the mother for permission to open drawers and closets, searching for a diary or personal items she might have kept. Permission was granted. Hezi and Itzik searched for anything indicating her state of mind but found nothing.

After half an hour, Hezi said to Itzik, "Let's go to the hostel where she stayed. We need to find a clue."

The two arrived at the hostel with determination. They presented their badges, requested to enter, and were granted permission. They met with the manager, Galia, in her office.

"We're conducting a covert investigation. Tell us everything you know about Noa Alush," Hezi asked.

"What happened to her?"

"She was murdered."

Galia looked shocked and horrified. "She stayed here for about a month two years ago. She was a bit odd, a loner, not very sociable. She always asked to eat alone."

"Who took care of her at the hostel?" Itzik asked.

"A guy named Raz Sela. He left a while ago."

"How can we reach him?" Hezi asked.

Galia gave them his contact details. "Could you give us a tour of the place so we can get an impression?"

"Of course."

The two arrived at Noa's room. Another girl was sitting on the bed, looking at them curiously. The room was tidy.

After the tour, they drove to Raz's house but didn't find him, so they returned to the police station.

Chapter 25

The next day, Hezi arrived at his office and found a sealed brown envelope on his desk. He stared at it for a while before gathering the courage to open it. Inside were the results of the samples he had taken from the forest. The DNA test revealed that the blood belonged to both the victim and another person: Raz Sela. Other findings from the scene also pointed to Raz as the primary suspect in the crime.

Itzik appeared at the office door. By now, Hezi was used to this and wasn't surprised to see him.

"Well, do we have a suspect?" Itzik asked curiously.

"Yes, it's the same guy whose house we visited yesterday."

"I guess he's disappeared. We'll need to find out where he's hiding."

"Yes, maybe with some relatives."

Itzik notified the receptionist at the front desk, requesting the dissemination of the suspect's photo and details among the police officers and the mobilization of a few patrol cars for the search.

"Let's go," he said to Hezi.

The two arrived at the home of the suspect's parents. They didn't expect to find Raz there, but they hoped to get significant information about his whereabouts. A man in his seventies opened the door, startled to see two policemen standing before him.

"How can I help you?" he asked, a hint of fear in his voice.

They identified themselves and showed their badges.

"Your son is suspected of murder, and we have a few questions for you," Itzik said, entering the house without asking for permission. Hezi followed him inside.

"My son? That can't be. He's a good person."

"Yeah, that's what they all say," Itzik replied, while Hezi stood by the living room cabinet, glancing at family photos, trying to learn more about the suspect's lifestyle.

Itzik sat on the sofa across from the old man and began bombarding him with questions. "When was the last time you saw him? Were your relations normal? Did he say anything suspicious?"

While Itzik conducted the questioning, Hezi wandered through the rooms, searching for incriminating clues. He returned to the living room. "Let's go. There's nothing here," he declared.

Itzik wrote his phone number on a piece of paper and handed it to the old man. "If you have any new information, contact me." He then rose from his seat, and the two left.

While driving, Hezi suggested breaking into Raz's home.

"We need a court warrant," Itzik responded, adding, "I'll take care of it."

Itzik called the station commander, Ron, updated him on the investigation, and requested that he handle the warrant. Within twenty minutes, approval was granted.

Itzik changed course and, while en route, called a locksmith to meet them at Raz's address. When they arrived, the locksmiths were already waiting for them.

"Doron, open the door quietly. We don't want the neighbors to notice," Itzik requested.

"I'm not sure how exactly I'll do that, but I'll try to be gentle," Doron replied.

The door was unlocked, and the locksmiths went on their way. Itzik and Hezi entered the apartment. Hezi went into the kitchen and saw leftover food on the table.

"He's still living here," Hezi murmured.

"Maybe we'll get lucky and catch him by surprise," Itzik replied, heading to the suspect's room. Hezi joined him.

The two opened the wardrobe and drawers but found nothing. Hezi looked under the bed and found a small box.

"Look what I found," he said, placing the box on the bed.

Hezi opened it and began rummaging through a collection of old memorabilia Raz had gathered, including old watches and toy cars. Suddenly, he noticed several relatively well-preserved, dusty photos.

"Look what I discovered," he said, showing them to Itzik. The pictures clearly showed Raz and Noa embracing.

"A crime of passion," Itzik remarked, looking satisfied.

Suddenly, the door opened, and footsteps were heard in the living room. Itzik glanced at Hezi. They both drew their guns and cautiously advanced toward the room's entrance. The footsteps retreated.

The two rushed to the living room and saw a man slipping out the front door.

"Stop!" Itzik shouted, sprinting after him, with Hezi close behind.

Thunder roared, and a torrential downpour began. Soaked, they scanned their surroundings and saw the figure disappearing between the buildings. They started running but soon lost sight of him. Itzik muttered a quiet curse, annoyed that the chase had failed.

"Let's find shelter from the rain," Hezi said to Itzik, and the two entered a nearby building.

Itzik called the station, requesting reinforcements and roadblocks in the area. Half an hour later, several patrol cars arrived and set up roadblocks in the city. Plainclothes officers roamed the streets, trying to spot the suspect, but he was nowhere to be found, as if the earth had swallowed him.

The rain began to let up. Itzik wanted to end the event, change his wet clothes, and have a hot drink.

"The suspect probably didn't get far. He's hiding from the rain and will soon come out and try to escape," Hezi said.

"What do you suggest?" Itzik asked, hoping to wrap things up as soon as possible.

"I suggest—"

Hezi's phone rang. He looked at the screen and saw Tamar's name.

"I can't believe it," he muttered, reluctantly answering the call.

"Yes, I don't have much time," he said impatiently.

"Why are there roadblocks in the city? Do you have something for me? I know you do."

"I have no information for you right now. If I do, I'll let you know.

"Don't forget," she said before hanging up.

"You'll have to tell your girlfriend, you know. Better sooner than later, even if it comes at a high cost. Otherwise, you'll always be dependent on her," Itzik said.

"You're right," Hezi replied, pausing to gather his thoughts. "Back to the matter at hand. I suggest we search the yards and under the staircases of the tall buildings."

"Good idea. Let's go," Itzik agreed.

First, they searched the stairwells of the buildings. Neighbors watched them suspiciously and curiously, with some gathering the courage to approach and ask what they were doing.

After more than an hour of searching with no results, the two abandoned the idea and entered the yards, scanning every possible hiding spot. In some homes, they were not welcomed warmly and had to explain their presence. In a few places, alarm systems went off when they entered, forcing them to explain themselves again.

In the yard of an old, run-down house, Hezi spotted a figure hiding beneath a rusty old car. He signaled to Itzik, who recognized the figure. The two drew their guns, splitting up and advancing toward him from both sides, never taking their eyes off him.

Hezi aimed his gun and ordered the man to come out of hiding. The man emerged with his hands raised, looking terrified.

They slowly approached him with their guns drawn.

"That's the suspect," Hezi confirmed after recognizing his face.

Itzik grabbed him, forcefully pulling his hands behind his back and handcuffing him. He then informed the police that the suspect was in custody.

Within a short time, a patrol car arrived and took the suspect away.

***

Hezi had been struggling for a long time with how to tell Keren about what had happened that fateful night at the hostel with Tamar. The decision weighed heavily on him. He knew he would pay a high price but secretly hoped it wouldn't be so costly as to lead to a breakup. Predicting Keren's reaction was hard, and he had already braced himself for the worst-case scenario. He mulled over different ways to break the news and tried to decide on the right moment to minimize the damage.

After dinner, when the atmosphere was calm and relaxed, Hezi decided the time had come. As they sat on the couch, he turned to Keren and said, with growing apprehension, "I have something important to tell you. I know it will sound really bad, but please try to understand before jumping to conclusions."

"What happened?" she asked, surprised.

Hezi began telling her the story. He tried to downplay the incident, claiming he had been forced into it and found it hard to resist under the circumstances.

Keren's mind started connecting the dots between the incident and Tamar's sudden appearance in their lives.

"That's why you told me to stay away from her, right?"

"Yes. I'm sorry for everything that happened. It was a one-time mistake, and it won't happen again, I promise."

"But it already happened," she replied angrily.

"I know. She means nothing to me. You're the only one I love."

"You should have thought of that before," she responded coldly, getting up and heading to the bedroom.

Hezi remained on the couch, trying to assess the damage. He followed her to the bedroom and found her packing a suitcase.

"Please stay," he pleaded. But Keren didn't respond. When she finished packing, she left the house, slamming the door behind her.

Hezi remained alone, staring at the door in a daze, hoping it might open again and Keren would return. But the door didn't open, and the weight on his heart only grew heavier. He felt lost and disconnected, his mind flooded with countless thoughts that threatened to drown him in a sea of tears lodged in his throat. He couldn't sleep at all that night.

A new day began, and Hezi struggled to get up and leave his empty bed. The darkness and silence closed in on him from all sides. His eyes were red from lack of sleep, and he found it hard to function or get ready.

He started his workday sitting idly for a long time, feeling increasingly overwhelmed, staring at the white walls as if searching for something hidden.

Itzik entered his office. "What's going on?" he asked, noticing Hezi's gloomy state.

"I told her, like you advised, and she left me."

"That was bound to happen; you didn't have much choice," Itzik tried to console him. "Come out with us tonight for a beer. You need to get out and clear your head. In the meantime, the suspect in the girl's murder, Raz, is waiting for us in the interrogation room."

"Alright, you handle the interrogation, and I'll step in if needed," Hezi requested, and Itzik agreed.

The two of them entered the interrogation room. Raz sat by the table in prison clothes, handcuffed at both his wrists and ankles.

Itzik began to speak, accusing Raz of the crime. Raz remained calm and denied the charges. At a certain point, Hezi lost his temper, slammed the file on the table, pointed at him, and said, "The DNA tests show beyond a doubt that you're the killer. The only thing I care about is the motive. We can sit here for days until you're so exhausted you'll beg to tell us, just so we'll leave you alone. Or you can tell us voluntarily and save us unnecessary time."

Raz lowered his gaze, realizing he had no way out.

"I was her caretaker. Over time, we developed a relationship, and I fell in love with her."

Hezi erupted in fury, interrupting him. "For God's sake, you were her caretaker! There's more than a twenty-year age gap between you two!"

Raz remained silent. "Go on," Itzik encouraged him.

"After she left the hostel, we kept seeing each other. I wanted her to move in with me, but she refused. Her parents opposed our relationship, and she wanted to break up. I couldn't let that happen."

"So, you just killed her?" Hezi accused him again.

Raz stayed silent once more.

"I didn't hear you!" Hezi shouted. "What did you want to say?"

"I took her to the grove and tried to convince her to change her mind, but she refused. I killed her in a fit of rage."

Hezi rose from his chair, moving toward him, ready to unleash his anger, but Itzik stopped him.

"Calm down," Itzik whispered.

"Now his lawyer will come, claim he's a normal guy from a good family, that he didn't mean to do it, and it was just temporary insanity," Hezi said as he sat back down.

Itzik called for the guards to take Raz back to his cell.

"Well, that's another case closed," Itzik said to Hezi as they left the room.

Hezi wasn't thrilled to go out that evening; he was sad and depressed. The loneliness only made it harder, leaving him to sit and stare at the walls, doing nothing.

Itzik insisted Hezi get out to clear his head. He showed up at Hezi's house and drove him to a crowded bar in the industrial area, where a few other officers were waiting, dressed casually. They looked cheerful, holding beers, and warmly welcomed them.

Hezi sat with them at the table, but he seemed disconnected. Itzik convinced one of the female officers, Liat, to keep him company and try to distract him from his troubling thoughts, and she was happy to do so.

The waiter arrived with a large tray and placed glasses of beer on the table. The officers drank, had fun, and seemed especially lively.

After one beer, Hezi felt a bit more relaxed and joked with his friends.

The night ended late, and Itzik drove Hezi back to his empty home.

The silence in the house brought back the feelings of loneliness and heaviness, but exhaustion overcame him, and he fell asleep fully clothed on the living room couch.

The week passed slowly, offering little relief. During the week, Hezi tried calling Keren several times, but she often quickly hung up or ignored the call. Summoning his courage, he drove to her parents' house with a bouquet of flowers and an apology letter. When he rang the doorbell, her mother opened the door and told him that

Keren didn't want to see him. He had no choice but to leave, just as he came.

Chapter 26

Hezi tried to keep himself busy at work until late at night to avoid being consumed by thoughts and despair. He learned to cook from recipes he found online. Once a week, he cleaned the house, watered, and tended to the plants Keren had bought. On weekends, when he was alone, he watched drama films, read a thick book on the meaning of life in the modern age, and occasionally listened to soothing music that he liked.

One evening, just before going to bed, he received an urgent call from Chief Superintendent Beniso, asking him to come to the station immediately. Hezi considered complaining that he hadn't had a chance to rest from his previous shift, but there was no point. The shifts were scheduled based on manpower availability and the urgency of events.

When he arrived at the station, he was informed that highly dangerous security prisoners had escaped from Rimon Prison in the north, and they needed to be found and returned before they could cause harm to the public.

"It's going to be a long night," Itzik said to him.

"Wait until the media finds out," Hezi replied.

"Yeah. They'll be all over us, demanding explanations."

"Explanations or excuses—you choose."

Beniso instructed the arriving officers to enter the briefing room. Hezi and Itzik walked in and sat in the second row.

Once the room was full and everyone was seated, Beniso entered and scanned the crowd.

"I see everyone's here," he said. "About two hours ago, according to the prison service's estimates, six highly dangerous security prisoners managed to escape and are likely heading toward the West Bank. They might be armed, they might have split into several groups, they might have had a car waiting for them, or they could be hiding nearby. We don't know anything for sure right now; it's all speculation. We must consider all possibilities and stay alert to the dangers. If you spot anything suspicious, contact the command post (CP) that we'll set up in the field. Any questions?"

The room remained silent.

"Good. Moshe will assign you to groups and equip you with flashlights and radios."

After being equipped, the officers set out. Hezi felt tense, knowing that the night ahead would be long and filled with unpredictable events.

When they arrived at the prison complex, they saw the K9 unit searching for any clues. Moshe gathered the officers near the northern part of the prison by the wall, pointed to a narrow opening, and said, "This is where the terrorists escaped. Your job is to find them and bring them back alive. Each group will sweep the area around the prison."

Hezi and Itzik were in a group of six officers. They walked along a gravel slope, shining their flashlights between the bushes, searching for anything suspicious. A pale moonlight faintly illuminated the abandoned trees swaying in the light breeze and the remote dirt paths they walked along.

Time passed quickly, but no new evidence was found. Suddenly, Hezi's phone rang. He quickly answered. It was Tamar on the other end.

"Yes," he whispered.

"I heard terrorists escaped from Rimon Prison. Do you have any information for me?"

"No, and even if I did, I wouldn't give it to you. Please don't call me again," he said.

"Be nice, and don't forget our little secret."

"You can tell whoever you want about it."

"Aren't you afraid Keren will find out?"

"She already knows, and she left me because of you," he said angrily and hung up.

Itzik overheard the conversation but chose not to intervene.

Hezi's team continued searching the area, thoroughly checking every bush, tree, and rock. Occasionally, the sounds of roaming jackals and barking stray dogs echoed in the distance. The rustling of bushes or an animal startled by their presence only added to the tension.

Suddenly, Hezi spotted distant lights.

"What's that?" he asked Itzik, pointing toward them.

"That's an Arab village," Itzik replied.

"Let's go there."

Itzik reported on the radio to the command post that the group was heading toward the village and might need reinforcements if things escalated.

"Okay. Just stay alert," came the reply.

The group reached a main road, crossed it, and entered the village. At this hour, the streets were empty, and everyone was inside their homes.

Hezi feared someone might come out, spot them, and cause a commotion, but nothing of the sort happened.

The group walked through the streets, listening carefully for any suspicious noises. Hezi thought it was hopeless to find someone hiding among the tightly packed buildings—like searching for a needle in a haystack.

They arrived at a crossroads, and Hezi stood still, considering the options ahead of them. Suddenly, he saw a truck parked near one of the less-lit houses.

"Let's go there," he said to Itzik, pointing toward the dark street.

As they approached the truck, they heard footsteps behind it.

Itzik signaled the officers to be quiet and prepare for any possible scenario. They drew their guns and shone their flashlights toward the truck.

The officers spotted one terrorist hiding underneath the truck. He looked frightened, thin, and gaunt.

Itzik signaled for him to come out with his hands raised, and he complied.

"Put the cuffs on him," Itzik ordered Hezi.

While Hezi was turning the prisoner around to handcuff him, a single burst of gunfire suddenly rang out. Hezi was hit and collapsed to the ground.

Yoni, another officer nearby, quickly cuffed the prisoner and took cover. The officers returned fire toward the source of the shots, killing another terrorist who had been hiding in the nearby bushes.

Itzik radioed the command post, reporting the incident and urgently requesting an ambulance.

"We have an officer down," he said.

"Who's injured?"

"Hezi."

Itzik rushed to Hezi in a panic, trying to assess the severity of the wound. The bullet had hit Hezi in the side and exited through the other side.

Itzik pressed his hand on the wound, trying to stop the bleeding. "Don't worry, I'm with you. Stay awake," he tried to reassure him.

Hezi had lost a lot of blood and groaned in pain. He closed his eyes and lost consciousness. An ambulance arrived shortly after, intubated Hezi, and rushed him to the hospital, where he was put on a ventilator and sedated.

Upon arrival at the hospital, Hezi was taken into surgery. His wounds were stitched up, bandaged, and he was moved to the recovery room for further monitoring.

***

Hezi slowly woke up, looking around curiously. He found himself lying alone in a hospital room and realized where he was. He didn't know how long he had been unconscious. This wasn't the first time he had lain helpless in a hospital bed, waiting for a nurse to visit and update him on his condition, but this time, there was no one to visit him, no one asking about his well-being. He looked exhausted, sad, and lonely.

Hezi was connected to an IV and painkillers. The room's lighting made it hard for him to fall back asleep, so he remained awake for about an hour until the doctor came in to assess his condition.

"What's my condition, doctor?" he asked.

"You'll survive. You've already survived worse. Someone up there must really like you," the doctor said with a smile.

The doctor checked his blood pressure and wrote something down in his medical chart.

"How long have I been here?" Hezi asked.

"Three days," the doctor replied and left.

Hezi tried to close his eyes. The background noise of other patients and visitors disturbed him, but his fatigue finally overpowered him, and he fell asleep.

In the evening, Itzik arrived to visit him, dressed in his police uniform.

"How are you?" he asked.

"I'm still in pain," Hezi replied.

"It'll pass. I wanted to update you that we caught all the escaped prisoners. They were returned to prison and will soon be on trial."

"Did they figure out how they escaped?"

"They dug a tunnel under the prison. One of the guards fell asleep in the watchtower and didn't notice the suspicious movement."

"That's a failure someone will pay for dearly."

"Not sure," Itzik said with a smile. "The prison authorities will probably deny responsibility, claiming that the escape was inevitable due to years of neglect in the prison conditions."

"You're probably right," Hezi replied, sinking into thoughts about avoidable failures that could have been prevented with better judgment.

"There's someone here who's been waiting to see you. It took me a while to convince her to come. It wasn't easy. I hope it's okay with you?" Itzik said.

Hezi was surprised; he knew it was Keren. He was curious how Itzik had managed to get her there, but he didn't have time to ask, as Itzik quickly left the room.

Keren entered, and Hezi looked more excited than ever. Itzik followed behind her. "I must go. I'll leave you two alone," he said with a smile and hurried out.

Hezi wanted to get out of bed, but the pain from his injury kept him lying down.

"I'm sorry for everything," he said. "I wish I could turn back time."

Keren sat down in the chair by his bed, staying silent.

"You can't turn back time," she finally said.

"Unfortunately, you're right," he replied.

For a moment, there was silence. Hezi was afraid that every word he said would only do more harm than good.

"So, how are you feeling?" she eventually asked.

"I'm in a lot of pain on my side," he said.

"It'll take time, but you'll recover."

"Yeah," he said, touching the painful area.

"You should know, I'm still hurt by you."

"I understand."

"My trust in you is badly damaged. You'll have to work hard to rebuild it."

"I'm willing to do whatever it takes."

Another moment of silence.

"Do you want something to drink? I'm going to get a juice from the vending machine."

"No, thanks."

When she returned, she sat down again and, to his surprise, asked, "I've been wondering, what are your plans for the future?"

"I want to get married and start a family."

"You can't keep working in the police, risking your life and leaving your partner in constant worry and uncertainty."

"I know. I'm going to go back to working in high-tech—three days from home and two in the office."

"You've thought it all through, I see."

"I've had plenty of time to think about everything."

"And what about your prophetic dreams?"

"I can't ignore them."

"I didn't expect you to."

"I guess I'll keep trying to help people in emergencies or distress without putting myself in danger."

Keren smiled and stood up. "I have to go."

"Will I see you again?" he asked.

"When are you getting discharged?"

"In a few days."

"Call me, and I'll come to pick you up," she said.

"Thank you for visiting me."

Keren smiled and left the room.

Hezi beamed with happiness, even though deep down he knew he had a long road ahead to win Keren's heart back.

The day of Hezi's discharge from the hospital finally arrived. The wound still hurt him, but the pain was bearable. A bandage covered the stitches from the bullet injury. He was still struggling with simple tasks, like sitting or standing on his own. He sat on the bed, patiently and excitedly waiting for Keren.

As promised, Keren arrived at the hospital in the early afternoon and entered his room.

"I feel like I've been reborn," he said to her.

"And it's not the first time," she added with a smile.

"Come on, I'll help you walk. You've got a long recovery ahead of you."

Milton Keynes UK
Ingram Content Group UK Ltd.
UKHW021925201124
451474UK00013B/932

9 798330 438105